NIMBUS:
The Creation Story
According To Mr. G.

IDHHB, INC. — DONEVE DESIGNS
PUBLISHERS
1978

Special thanks to the *Second Foundation.*

ISBN: 0-89556-008-9
Library of Congress Catalog Number: 78-58330

Editor's Note

Long suppressed and nearly lost forever, this *Fourth-Way* novel in many ways surpasses the material released earlier. Unlike the theatrical, complex sentence-construction of Orage, and Nicoll's pedagogery, we have chosen a modern, straightforward approach, although still not in any way a "bon-ton" literary style, feeling that the material itself is sufficiently complex without additional artifical language difficulties.

In the original versions such difficulties were not present. G's manuscript, when read in his own tongue, was neither devious nor obtuse. Only in translation into other languages such problems arise.

In this version for American and English audiences, we have updated some material, in modern settings where they are necessary to maintain the tone and spirit of the original.

The publication of this exceptional work has long been awaited by students of the Fourth Way. We hope that it provides something profitable for your being.

A Note From The Author

This book is intended to be read in several very definite stages:

First — as if this book were an ordinary novel; that is, the reader ought to read the material for the first time just trying to get the sense of the work in an ordinary way.

Second — read the book in a group, and listen to the sounds of the words, allowing the words to evoke images in your mentation.

Third — read each paragraph for a "hidden" meaning or sense and have discussions among the group as to what these might be, whether they are literary, anagrammatic, puns, or whatever secondary sense you might discover.

Fourth — read the book as if it were describing stages of development; as if it were an engineering manual or a map of stages of consciousness that could be followed.

Fifth — only now should you begin to try to find the seven levels of meaning of each paragraph and chapter, and put them together in a matrix pattern. This effort should be made under supervision and guidance of an initiated individual, but an unguided group can receive inner guidance if sincere in effort and spirit. There are seven levels of understanding in each story, and also to each apartition or paragraph relating to the inner and outer life of humanity. There is also a chapter on the three bodies of man, but this is hidden within other material, and can only be uncovered by attempting to use this information in a practical way.

Contents

1   Sinai Memorial Mountain 3

2   Ladies Of Istanbul. 14

3   Origins Of Harold 16

4   Harold And The Hag 21

5   The Fifth Century 25

6   The Companions 29

7   The Big Secret. 35

8   How To Be A Giant 38

9   The Mysterious Stranger 40

10   A Happy Reunion 45

11   Power-How To Get It And Use It. 49

12   In The Dungeon 51

Contents

13 How Humans Think And Why They Go Mad 55

14 The Turning Point............................60

15 Building The Fake Giant 62

16 The Law Of Agriventakiolno 70

17 Empty Bags With Walls Of Skin.................72

18 Attack Of The Villagers 84

19 The Aftermath...............................89

20 First Descent On Gnaripogipog 91

21 The Country Of Nakhnik 103

22 What Happened To Harold? 107

23 The Lord's Last Gasp 111

24 The Pan-Angelic Conference...................119

25 Return Of The Lord..........................121

26 The Second Day 124

27 The Lord Explains Some Of The Problem 126

28 The Fourth Day Of The Pan-Angelic Conference 136

29 The Fifth Day Of The Pan-Angelic Conference......149

30 The Sixth Day Of The Pan-Angelic Conference 156

31 The Seventh Day Of The Pan-Angelic Conference ...160

32 Hot On The Trail............................168

33 The Lord's Explanation Of It All.................172

NIMBUS

CHAPTER ONE

Sinai Memorial Mountain

It was Burning Bush Time once again on Mount Sinai, and I had wandered along the dusty, winding road to the top of the mountain where Our Lord had built a tiny tourist shop in order to derive at least some small benefit from His otherwise completely unprofitable enterprise regarding a certain 'Mr. Moses' some time before this.

I stood uncertainly in front of His tent, flipping a coin enabling me to find time to work up the nerve to open the flap and go inside.

I had figured to magic a free meal out of Him — The Old Man always was an easy touch — but knowing the kind of food He was very likely to serve — too much on the gourmet side for my taste — I wasn't sure I could stomach the results, this in spite of the dismal fact that it had been several days now and I still had not been able to scrape together the wherewithal for a hot meal.

My growling gut had just won the argument when Archangel Mike sauntered up within the shadow outside Our Lord's tent — a total copy of the scene using a double of the housing from the silent film, *The Sheik*, with Rudolph Valentino — and as we stood there, he gave me a look implying he knew something I didn't know...and probably would not like to find out.

"Why, Archangel Gabriel," he almost spat but skillfully cooed, "I didn't know you still go in for gourmet food."

"What do you mean?" I asked, trying to strangle the slight hint of terror creeping into my normally calm and unruffled voice.

"I mean just that He knew you were coming to visit — of course — and prepared a special treat for you...your favorite dish."

"Oh, no, not again!" I moaned. "He wouldn't do this to me. He *knows* how I hate that stuff!"

"Maybe now you'll stop bumming free meals, Gabriel," Mike said gleefully. "Yes, indeed...*Lambs' eyes tonight* — especially for you!" He waited a moment, only long enough to see the effect of his little announcement...then he shambled off into the angels' compound.

"I hate it," I muttered, "I hate them and *He* knows it — He *knows* I can't stand lambs' eyes," my words ran after Mike's retreating form. "They *pop* when you bite into them!" I finally shouted. He was about twenty feet away before he turned around.

"Really?" he asked with an innocent air. "Perhaps now it's time for you to get a job, Gabriel."

"Like what?" I asked. "Who's hiring Archangels these days?"

"Well, then, you might as well go on in," he said. "Too late to back out now. He doesn't like to be kept waiting."

Knowing he was right, I ducked into the tent realizing it was hopeless...I couldn't forget what was to be my dinner. I had a wild hope...if I could keep Him talking all night, He'd forget about the food, and when He realized it had gotten cold, (there's no way to properly re-heat lambs' eyes) He'd take me out for a hamburger and fries or something. I had to keep Him talking.

The inside of the tent was decorated about the way I

expected — *early French Bordello.* It was a bit surprising to find Our Lord manifesting as an old man. His usual was a pillar of fire or a burning bush. In any case, I had never seen Him appear as anything less thermal than a *crepe suzette.* "No burning bush? Not even the pillar of fire?" I asked.

"Aaaahhh," He exclaimed in a disgusted tone, "I been getting a continual entropic decrease of three-point-two times ten to the twenty-second power *joules* per degree, every damn year since Newton discovered the fig," He complained bitterly.

"The fig?" I was puzzled.

"Physics," He explained. "Energy drain. Einstein made it worse. Sit down...Here's a comfortable cushion," He said, motioning me to a place close to Him.

I sat down as He spoke, looking wildly about for any evidence of a 16mm film projector. I couldn't help but feel apprehensive that He might insist on showing *Ben Hur* once again. He always told anyone who had never met His skinny, dark-haired son that He looked *exactly* like Francis X. Bushman. However, I didn't see any movie equipment and, feeling somewhat reassured, leaned back against the pillow, nodding politely in formal greeting.

It has always been the custom of the Heavenly Host to nod toward each other as a token of respect but, now that I've been cogitating, it seems that lately The Lord has been thinking of instituting the custom of genuflecting, since the Pope gets it from his people, and The Lord is of the opinion that He ought to receive at least as much respect as the Pope of Italy.

He is pretty miffed that, among human beings — and even among angels, some who shall remain nameless — He gets less respect than they give to Johnny Weismuller, John L. Sullivan, John Barrymore and John Wayne. For a while, He gave serious consideration to changing His name to John.

It might have helped. I was with Him once when He sneezed, and I didn't know what to say.

"Well, we can sit around here in this Ay-rab tent, Gabriel," He said in His best 'Will Rogers' drawl. "By the way...Have I mentioned that this is the same exact tent used in the silent film, *The Sheik*, with Rudolph Valentino? Archangel Mike says that I do look a little like Valentino when the light is right. Do *you* think I look like Valentino?" He asked me in a threatening tone.

The light must not have been just right, because if He looked like Valentino, so did Peter Lorre.

"Yes, Lord, exactly like Valentino."

"Well, thanks, Gabriel." He said. "Say, I just had a thought — you ever see *Ben Hur*? Of course, we showed that last Xmas, didn't we? Anyway, we can sit around here yakking about all kinds of things, but if you got any stories about the humans here on Earth, I'd like to hear them."

"Oh, Lord," I said. "I know all kinds of stories about the goings-on at Galactic Center, but I don't know a whole lot about these humans at all," I replied, as expected. (You don't tell The Lord anything about His own creations. He likes to spin the stories Himself, so the sooner you discover that about Him, the better you and He will get along. Besides, how can you tell someone who knows *everything*, a story He hasn't heard before?)

"So — you want to know about them, eh?" He asked. So far, my plan to avoid lambs' eyes seemed to be working.

"Yes, Lord. I would like especially to understand the causes of their strange destructive behavior toward each other and toward their harmless and benevolent planet," I temporized, knowing how *that* would get Him cranked up on the subject.

"Son of a blank, you are right, Gabriel!" He said. "As it turns out, there is nothing else in the Great Megalocosmos — or even in the Studio on the Planning Board for next year's rides — nearly approximating them. But, by now you must already be quite aware of the various reasons for their odd attitudes which force them to rush headlong into the total destruction of all life on their planet?''

''No, Lord. Although I am, of course, aware of several of their peculiarities, there has not yet been formed within my mentation and general presence sufficient evidential data to create the required *All-Understanding-Comprehension* regarding the actions of humans from which I could obtain a definite result regarding their causes.''

''Oh.'' It was obvious The Lord had not understood a single word I had said. ''I can send for the food, if you're bored with the subject,'' He offered.

''Lord, you know very well that I meant that I was profoundly interested,'' I said hoarsely, with just a hint of desperation.

''Of course, of course. Certainly I did. I was simply testing you, to see if you knew what you meant.''

''Yes. Please, Lord, tell me more about them.''

''So — you want to hear about these *hairless monkeys* calling themselves 'men' and 'women', eh?''

''*Exactement*, Lord.''

''Well, I'll get on with it, then.'' He said, quite simply.

''Oh, wonderful, Lord!'' I replied. ''Now I have the opportunity to understand all the data in my own experience with humans and, as a result, I will be able to satisfy not only my curiosity regarding them, but also thanks to this, I will be more able to perform my work effectively when among them. Not only that, but I will be able to imitate their behavior more closely, thus avoiding the unfortunate results obtained by so many messengers sent previously to this third planet of the solar system *Ors*.''

''Are you going to let me tell the story, or aren't you?'' He seemed petulant.

Aware, now, that I might have gone too far in expressing joy, I immediately lapsed into a Quiet-Listening-Attitude

Satisfied that He seemed to have my devoted attention,

The Lord continued, "I thought it might be useful in the beginning to give you some background on a few of my activities here on the planet Earth by recounting some of my early experiences with man, most especially regarding his creation and purpose for existing. I mean, of course, his *real* purpose — not what he seems to imagine for himself. This should give you the exact sequence of data — in reverse, of course, as it should be — regarding the cause of man's irritating stupidity and ignorance. Not only that but, in the meantime, it will help me to crank up my thoughts, which have been out of use for some time."

"You mean you haven't talked about this lately, Lord?"

"Of course not, Gabriel. How many angels do you think I could interest in such an obscure subject as humans?"

"It depends, Lord. It does depend. How many of them are out of work?"

"What?"

"Nothing, Lord. Go on with what you were saying."

"Hmmph. Before I tell you how I came to do what I did, and how humans came to be what they are as a result of what I did, I want to warn you that I won't, under any circumstances, tolerate outbursts of laughter — unless I also laugh — regarding these efforts of mine to create within a basically unconscious universe, a genuinely self-arising conscious being. And since you angels are only the results of one of my earliest — and maybe now in retrospect not completely successful — efforts, I won't accept the slightest giggle from you. A lot of stuff turned out all right and, besides, without humans, everything would be so serious. Can you imagine how boring it would be, if everything in the universe went according to plan? I'd have nothing to do but wait until it all ran down again."

The Lord sat back a little, in order to better pose against the huge velvet pillow. With great concentration, he carefully selected a cigarette out of a silver case inscribed with *The Lord He Done It...From The Angelic Host*, and just as carefully inserted the long cigarette into an amber cigarette holder. The holder was just a fraction too small to accept the cigarette easily and, after struggling with it for a moment, The Lord threw both items past the tent flap onto the ground outside. He then continued His narrative as if nothing had happened.

"It is interesting to me, Gabriel," The Old Man said, "that within the psyche of humans, stowed away behind a bulkhead or something, there is a mysterious force that, just about the time they are trying their best to be gentlemen and gentlewomen, will invariably tiptoe out in its *Astral Dr. Dentons* and clip somebody or other on the left ear. In short, while under ordinary conditions they may seem just like roses, roses — at the first sign of stress, they manage to become the biggest twitches you ever seen."

The Lord slapped His hands on His knees to illustrate that He had made an important point. "There is nothing too destructive or hostile for them to casually manifest toward one another, Gabriel. Not only toward each other, but also toward their planet which, from the viewpoint of higher gradations of reason, has done nothing to deserve their resentment. But from a human viewpoint it has committed the unpardonable sin of supporting them and providing their atmosphere, food, impressions, air, and also, as a bonus not required of nature, allowed the means for the formation of higher being bodies...should they wish to make use of immortality for the completion of their souls.

"It is a fact that these peculiar beings will not, under any circumstances, harm a hair on the head of a being who undermines them, victimizes them and works for their certain destruction and, in general, treats them as nothing more than fertilizer for the future use of the planet. On the other hand, they will try their best to destroy any being who works to free them from hostility and fear, and who performs service for the common good. Should one labor intentionally among them for the development in them of the means for conscious life, they without a single twinge of remorse, instantly take the required action needed to bring about the termination of the organism of any being who threatens them with the possible end of suffering. In short, they invariably crucify the offender."

"That's *funny*, Lord." I managed to suppress my laughter.

"Maybe *you* see the humor in it, Gabriel," He replied, taking a sip of His martini. "However, in no way, do I. These humans continually kill off my messengers. It is becoming more obvious to me now that they are still loused up from the effects of their third, extra brain."

"I don't understand, Lord. Why did you give them an extra brain?"

"The idea seemed sure-fire at the time. They ought to, as a result of this little invention of mine, make an effort to perceive the Real World."

"I still don't understand, Lord."

"This third brain prevents the perception of the Real World. It substitutes imaginary perception, and creates a world of the psyche, rather than of pure perception. You would think that, as soon as they discovered its existence, humans would have taken steps to eliminate this third and useless brain."

"What would that have accomplished?"

"By trying to eliminate the third brain — and hopefully succeeding — they would have made the exact efforts needed for the attainment of conscious life! They would otherwise never make these efforts in the ordinary course of human existence, and so would never be able to attain it."

"And they didn't do it the way you expected?"

"No. They *like* the extra brain. They use it to solve problems, and to create more problems to solve. They call it *the mind*. Now that I see the result, I undoubtedly have given them one brain too many. Why are they not grateful for this chance given to them by me? Instead of making efforts to eliminate this third brain — as I instructed when I implanted it — they use it to explain and excuse their irrational behavior.

"And while they at present, go to gathering places on at least one day each week...a day *late*, I might add — to express in prayer their appreciation for my efforts toward them — I *hope* it's to express appreciation — do you think they would continue to do so, if they knew that I was the party responsible for the placement of this third brain in their already crowded and chaotic bodies?

"There you have it, Gabriel — the chief cause of my growing resentment toward humans of the planet Earth. Even after all my efforts on their behalf and, after having given them specific instructions on how to get off this slaughterhouse planet of theirs — and, after all my careful planning for their transformation into conscious life, *they still refuse to evolve*. But, like I always say, not every effort can be a crackerjack!"

I knew He was going to say that. I had heard *that* chestnut so many times before. First, it was *Not every effort can be a crackerjack!* when we noticed the 'little miscalculation' that caused the disappearance of the continent Atlantis. Then He said it when we had the Red Sea Mishap. The truth of the matter is that He had actually been trying to drown Moses. We had to write a book to cover the error. Again a 'slight miscalculation' on His part. Then there's the thing that happened to His Son. He's forever explaining that one.

I remember Jesus saying, "They'll never get *me* up on one of those things."

"Yes," The Lord repeated to Himself, as I came out of my reverie, "Not every effort can be a crackerjack..." He gave a sigh, indicating that He also had been reminiscing about the incident. "Anyhow, I wanted to tell you a story."

I felt instantly relieved. For a moment I had thought that He might want to sing a song.

"This story is loaded with data about humans and you are going to like it," His tone implied I had *better* like it.

"It is filled with numerous examples of the peculiar psychic makeup of humans. Just by hearing it, you are bound to get a clear understanding of them. Even they — who are usually unappreciative of any of my efforts — are certain to like my story...that is to say, they probably would like it *if* they were going to hear it...Which they won't, Gabriel, unless, of course, you, in a moment of indiscretion, report this conversation to them."

"Lord," I protested, "you know how discreet I am."

"Nevertheless, if the humans of the planet Earth *do* hear this story — and I have an increasing suspicion that they *will* — and they don't like it, then it can only be attributed to the fact that they have not actualized within themselves the means for perfecting data and impressions from the Real World received by their beings. On the other hand, it could also be as a result of the interaction between the effects of the ingestion of a substance called by them 'baby food,' made by mass production methods in factories.

"In short, as a direct result of these influences on them in their early formatory years, when the psyche was vulnerable to such intervention, even though, in a healthy psyche, no such influence ought to be permanent or to cause more than temporary suffering in an individual, some of these impressions remain crystallized in their psyches even far beyond the time allotted for their full development into mature and responsible adults, and that is why some humans, without making a conscious decision about it one way or the other and, irregardless of the real data regarding their ingestion, like beets, while some prefer cabbage."

He took a deep breath before continuing. "Now, about this story I was going to tell you, Gabriel — I should mention at least some of the data proceeding in the hero's inner world and how it made up the reality of his being — what there was of it.

"And among all the stuff presented to you by me, which I learned quite by chance — especially those things regarding man's inner life — you will have enough data, and maybe even more than enough, to be able to decide for yourself the causes of the strange psyches of humans, Gabriel, although I got to caution you, don't be hasty. Do not draw any conclusions about them until all the facts are in."

CHAPTER TWO

Ladies Of Istanbul

"It was during the time I used to hang out with some certain young — but by no means without great power — ladies of the *Boringel* faith, who had their habitations in the great city of Istanbul, which is now Constantinople — or is it the other way around?

"And thanks to my interest in those inner-world principles which had been *aroused* in them after reaching near maturity, they performed, for my elucidation, the most amazing *Sacred Gymnastics* with me in their temples — called, *cheap hotels;* all for the purpose of demonstrating to me certain religious truths of theirs aimed at the Essences of men young and old.

"Aimed not only at their Essences, but also at their wallets, due to certain beliefs constated by these young ladies regarding the practice of their religion, that it could not be performed by them without — as obvious to any practitioner of their religion — the direct participation of a 'male member' of the congregation.

"And since in their opinions and beliefs now firmly rooted in them — if you will pardon the expression — through the influence of many 'full-page advertisements' in American film magazines, containing purported pronouncements by admired movie stars, no male member would participate in their unique religious practices unless these ladies altered in certain definite ways their ordinary outer manifestations, which are considered by humans much more important for the determination of 'objective relative importance of the individual' than the inner reality of Being — by the application of certain processed secretions of animals resulting from the activation of glands ordinarily reserved for their own reproductive processes, which are removed *post-mortem* and afterward chemically mixed so that they can be placed strategically on specific warm spots upon the female body of these religious beings.

"Moreover, these religious ladies of Istanbul — or is it Constantinople? — believed firmly that without certain fabrics arranged in a particular way upon their otherwise quite ordinary bodies in a style determined by a close relative of the 'drama critic', which daringly expose certain very definite fatty tissues according to the latest fashion craze in Hollywood and 'in Vogue', the said male members would not respond to them in a manner appropriate to their religious needs.

"And since these *Processed-Results-From-The-Unauthorized-Removal-Of-Otherwise-Perfectly-Healthy-Glands* and *Slinky-Garments-Designed-To-Stimulate-The-Ordinarily-Apathetic-Reproductive-Urges-Of-Human-Males* were so expensive to purchase, these tender and loving young religious ladies, practicing the results of their beliefs not only in the aforementioned temples but also on the streets, in automobiles and in the balconies of theaters, were forced to ask for a small donation from the congregation which they served.

"In short, they depended upon my intervention, and at every possible opportunity I responded to their prayers.

"It was during one of these responses to prayer that I heard from one of these religious ladies — the story of a man calling himself 'Harold of Cummingood.'"

CHAPTER THREE

Origins Of Harold

"According to her story, he was a former inhabitant of the Island of *Marakhugh*, which had, up until a few years earlier than this, been inhabited only by a breed of four-legged animals called *chorkodani* but, by the time of this story, it had long since become overrun by another animal, this time of biped variety.

"The wilder variety of humans had become firmly entrenched on the little island. When they ran out of grazing land on one end of the island, they went to the other end, enslaving the former inhabitants of the other end of the island.

"Finally, when they ran out of food altogether and, the island itself was unable to produce sufficient food for the native population, they began to import from other countries food and other items necessary for their existence.

"Eventually, because they did not produce raw materials of their own, they felt forced to annex these other countries to their own, and simply take what they needed for themselves.

"As a result of this *process-of-annexation*, they were also compelled for reasons far beyond their control, to eliminate certain inhabitants of these countries who opposed the said annexation.

"As a further result of this action of theirs to insure their own island's survival at the expense of other nations and the people inhabiting them, certain changes occurred in the psyches of the inhabitants of this little, but powerful, island community.

"That is to say, they became, at least on the inside, *Raving-Candidates-For-The-Lunatic-Asylum*. But if, on the inside they were in reality savage and butcherous, on the outside they seemed refined, serene, and respectable in every regard other than on the question of colonial independence.

"Because of this they developed an urgent wish to conceal their inner state of brute savagery, and so were compelled to create for themselves an artificial layer of civilized respectability for the outside, which resulted in the necessity for certain corrective institutions in their culture, which trained their young to maintain the appearance of gentleness and peaceful passivity, while perfectly concealing — at least to themselves — their real inner bestiality.

"And some of these crazes of theirs invented for the enhancement of their outer artificial personalities included *fashion, art, chess and checker clubs, top hats and tails, horse racing, hunting, shooting, country squires, titled gentry, boating, skiffing, soccer, squash, rugby, public schools* and many other similar inventions designed to take attention away from the inner being and place it as firmly as possible on the outer manifestation of the personality...

"Wait! Wait! In all of this, I have somehow forgotten to mention the most important invention of all of these — the *bowler hat, school tie* and *black umbrella*. There — now I think I have named them all.

"No, there is yet another factor of theirs in which our hero, Harold of Cummingood, was an expert and fanatic.

"This last craze, so popular among the said inhabitants of the little island of *Marakhugh* had been adopted readily by Harold of Cummingood. It is the deliberate *creation-of-reverence-for-now-living-persons-according-to-the-degree-of-*

importance-attained-by-certain-long-dead-ancestors.

"With the fanatical interest then common among these island-dwellers for such pursuits, Harold began at a very early age to collect his own personal list of dead persons who had been famous or power-possessing in the past, and with a few *deft twists of the pen*, managed to connect them somehow with his own familial lineage.

"He collected in this way a great many ancestors not genuinely his own and, in fact, not even faintly connected to anyone he knew.

"But as soon as he managed to connect the names of these ancestors to his own, he immediately traced their real connections up to the present day and, by simply using their family crest on his stationery, he would immediately write them a note, inviting himself to all family functions, requesting that they also provide for him a box at the opera and a seat at the horse-races.

"In this way he managed to live for some time without having to spend a single penny on his daily upkeep. Not only was he given breakfast, lunch and dinner at a different 'family seat' each day but, as a result of his imaginary membership in this special club of titled gentlemen and gentlewomen, he also managed to *get on the fiddle*...which meant that he received a special pension issued to all special people whose ancestors were either royal, famous or infamous. This is given to these modern special persons on the understanding that it would demoralize the masses to see the nobility working at common labor.

"Rather than demoralize the masses, this specially dispensed fund is given to each nobleperson by the state. Also, in order to protect the delicate sensibilities of the masses, these same genteel men and women are given only such jobs as would be suitable. That is, they are employed in The Admiralty, Foreign Office and House of Lords — which said jobs ruthlessly require them to report once every week, to collect a 'cheque for their services.'

"In short, they are paid handsomely to stay as much as possible out of the affairs of everyday life.

"Things would have gone on indefinitely for Harold, had he not made one small error in his calculations.

"He had never been completely satisfied with his name, which up to this time had been 'Harold Cummins-Goody-Goody'. It sounded too modern and also — due to the hyphenated surname which reminded him all too bitterly of his own hyphenated inner being — did not correspond to the image of himself which he wished to impress upon all those with whom he had daily contact.

"And so, in accordance with this 'Science of Genealogy', he changed his name to 'Harold of Cummingood', which sounded to him like a name that would have been right and proper for a Lord of the Fifth Century.

"But, unfortunately for him, it did not sound like a proper name to his noble and titled friends...and so...after a little investigation — kept very quiet by all concerned — his name was dropped from the registry of titled persons.

"Even though Harold had altered his name in strict accordance with the 'Law of Trees' — first discovered by the Druids as they gathered parasites from the lower branches of oaks, and there was seldom an investigation of a claim of ancestry since, to question one is to question all and, in a general investigation, it might be discovered that so many bold and noble ancestors could never have existed, not even from the dawn of time, and that moreover, if so many nobles *had* managed to achieve fame and power at the expense of the helpless peasantry, it would have required no smaller than a *Number Seven Bottomless Pit* to hold them all — he had made a serious error in choosing a new name.

"This error made by Harold in the choice of a new name in taking the name appropriate only to a Lord of the Fifth Century, rather than of the Twentieth, was due to his urgent need to identify with those people of the earlier period.

"Although he would appear outside his apartments in

garments appropriate to the modern world, when he was
alone in his flat he would remove these modern clothes and
put on ancient armor which he had been secretly collecting
and which had suspicious areas filed off the insides — which
corresponded exactly, had Harold been at all interested — to
the precise area required for the addition of the notice 'Made
in Japan'. In short, Harold was what is called a *Closet King*.

"It was in this way that Harold lost forever the only means
that he knew for earning a livelihood among the inhabitants
of the tiny island of *Marakhugh*. He was in fact so
embarrassed by the entire incident that he felt forced to
remove himself from the island and emigrate to America.

"And so he demonstrated that, in the great tradition of
nobility, he had a wonderful feeling and sense regarding
dead people, but little aptitude for dealing with living ones."

CHAPTER FOUR

Harold And The Hag

"When Harold left his accustomed domicile on the island of *Marakhugh,* and was compelled — in his opinion — to settle on the Continent America, he began — as a result of his feelings of inadequacy, resulting from a lowered social status, besides the suffering felt by him as a result of working at a regular job rather than simply periodically collecting a cheque — to develop a rather peculiar formation in his psyche.

"Unusual for us, that is, Gabriel. But not at all unusual in the ordinary life of the ordinary humans on Earth. Certainly it had become well-advanced in Harold's case, due to the earlier practice of wearing Fifth Century armor around his apartments, and pretending — rather well, for an ordinary human being — to have been a Lord of the Fifth Century.

"In short, this particular form of imagination dominated all his typical daily life now, during which he rigidly maintained his fantasy that he was in fact a Lord of the Fifth Century.

It was particularly impressive to me that he was able to maintain this illusion even riding the subway train underneath the city of Manhattan in New York on the

Continent America. He was able to make his way through the turnstile, drop in a coin and, get on a train, while completely maintaining this image.

"He maintained this daydream so well that he never saw the worn black patent-leather toe of an elderly lady's shoe until a few moments after he had ground his steel-tapped heel onto it. Even then he would perhaps never have been aware of this, except that the recipient of his offense caused him to come out of his reverie.

"Hey, you clumsy son of a banana!" she screamed in a piercing screech, "You just stepped on my toes!"

Suddenly, Harold did come out of his fantasy. "I sincerely apologize, madam, for having inconvenienced you in any way."

"Too late!" she screamed. "Now how am I going to carry my shopping bags?" she yelled, as she smashed them against his abdomen to demonstrate her utter helplessness.

"Harold did not wish to make a scene, and so he placated her by offering to carry them up to her apartment. But, when they got to the door of her apartment, he suddenly recalled all the stories he had heard about the tricks and confidence games that city dwellers play on unsuspecting *rubes*.

"What manner of hustle is this, madam?" he firmly inquired of her.

"I am the Hag of Eternity, Harold, and this was the only way I could get you up here without letting everyone know who I am."

"Why did you lure me up here?" Harold wanted to know.

"Because you obviously belong in the Fifth Century, not the Twentieth, if I am any judge at all," she answered.

"Harold was shocked. Up to this very moment, he had believed no one else in the entire universe to be privy to his inner life yet, seemingly, this one was knowledgeable about all. He decided to go along with her for awhile, thinking that, if what she had been saying were true, his suffering was now to be ended.

"In less than a flash, her door opened. Inside her Greenwich Village apartment sat a Persian cat staring at them from an overstuffed chair as they came through the entry.

"Across the room, on the other side of the overstuffed chair, a crystal ball blared out with voices and music. The Hag turned the volume down a little, so they could hear each other talk.

"Why don't you just turn it off?" demanded Harold.

"Off...off?" her voice rose plaintively, "You can't turn *that* darn thing off. If you want to, you can turn the volume up or down...or you can change the image...or you can adjust the color. But you can't turn it *off.*"

"Harold had no idea why anyone would want such a device in the first place. He had only asked about it because it interfered with his concentration and intention of hearing what the old woman was going to say about the Fifth Century, so that he could become, as he had desired for ever so long, to be a Lord of the Fifth Century.

"Without a further word regarding Harold's urgent wishes, the old woman walked over to the comfort chair, allowing the cat to climb into her lap, and sat down with a sigh of relief. Harold now could see himself in the crystal, parading about in ancient armor, and yelling something or other. The sound was too low for him to clearly understand — even though it was his own voice.

Trying desperately to cringe into a corner of his being, he broke out into an icy sweat. "I knew somebody was watching me. I could feel it," he told her. "How much do you want to keep this quiet?" he asked.

"This is not extortion, sweetie," she replied. "Look more closely — "

"That is not a modern city," he said, his voice more relaxed. "It looks like a scene from a long time ago."

"It is," she said.

"But why is everyone so little, and why am I so big

compared to them?'' he asked. "Oh, I get it — those are the
little people, elves and fairies — and I am among them!''

"No, those are ordinary people,'' she said. "Somehow, in
that time, you become a giant.''

"How do I do that?'' Harold wanted to know.

"*Because you get that way*," she explained, in a tone
reminiscent of Aimee Semple MacPherson trying to explain
her income tax return to a treasury agent.

"But I don't understand,'' Harold's vocal chords seemed
constricted.

"Of course,'' she agreed. "If you understood, you would
not have come here to go to the Fifth Century! Now,
however, it is time for you to go — except for a half hour in
which time we could ball while we are waiting for the time
machine to warm up. How about it, big boy?'' she enunciated
slowly.

*　　*　　*　　*　　*　　*

"Precisely, a half an hour later, the old hag led him up to a
wire mesh cage surrounded by huge electrodes and
humming boxes that glowed slightly in the darkened room
which they had entered through a secret panel in the
bathroom.

"The hag maneuvered Harold into the cage, and punched
a red button. Everything began to float. Harold felt a ripple
go through his body as if it were a piece of paper flapping in
the breeze.''

CHAPTER FIVE

The Fifth Century

"Harold rubbed his eyes, not at all certain that the old hag had somehow done it.

"Has she really sent me back?" he wondered, aloud. "It seems more like Central Park in New York City."

"He rubbed his eyes some more until they cleared up. When he could see better, he realized that, indeed, he was in Central Park in New York City. He broke out in a cold sweat, figuring that the old dame must have rolled him for eight bucks and left him to hatch out near the duck pond above Columbus Circle.

"Oh — sorry, dearie!" came an ephemeral voice from above. "Machine's miswired again." Everything went hazy again and, when his environment solidified, Harold found himself standing in the midst of a forest that agreed more with his expectations.

"A young lad was standing not ten feet away from him when he appeared. Harold could now see that he was on a path that led through the forest and more than likely eventually came to some sort of town.

"It *really is* the Fifth Century, Lord Cummingood," the boy told him with a disarming smile.

"What made you say that?" Harold asked in a suspicious tone, certain that he not only had been duped by the old hag but by this boy, as well.

"You looked as if you wanted to know " the boy reassured him, disappearing into a nearby birch tree.

"Harold was by now burning with curiosity about the scene revealed to him by the Hag of Eternity. He could not imagine how he would become a giant. According to his relative size in relation to the trees and to the young boy he had just seen — or had he? Perhaps this was all a hallucination — after all, he was still the normal size for a human being.

"How would he get to be giant-sized here in the Fifth Century? He wondered. He had already accepted that he had been somehow transported back through time. Harold resolved not to rest until he solved the mystery.

"He sat down and pondered the question. Gland Problem? Change of diet? Exercise?

"That he could not solve the problem so surprised him — in accordance with the psyche current among modern humans — they believe themselves to be able to solve anything with the use of this 'third brain' given to them by me — that he took a solemn vow not to rest until he discovered, and perhaps even learned to apply to himself, the *secret of gianthood.*

"Harold began walking slowly along the path without wondering — even for a moment, again in accordance with that peculiar psyche of theirs which instantly forgets forever any data which does not conform with their present understanding of reality — where the boy had gone.

."Had he solved that little riddle, he would have been able to complete his quest right then and there. But he kept walking, and as he walked, his pace quickened and he immersed himself in deep thought regarding the secret of gianthood which he now was certain must exist.

"The path soon led out of the woods, but not to a town at

first, as Harold saw as soon as he emerged from the trees. Before him, spread over the landscape, was a meadow and a large wooden building — a Thane Hall, as he knew from his studies of the period.

"Getting suddenly as if from out of nowhere the idea of enlisting others in his aid, and also hoping that these daring nobles — real living ancestors of the mild-mannered Twentieth-Century nobles — were no doubt just waiting for a new adventure and would be only too happy to go with him on his quest for gianthood, and would know better than he how to respond to an emergency in this time period — that is, they would protect him — he strode unhesitatingly up to the big building.

"He threw aside the large leathery hides which had been stretched across the doorway, and stepped firmly into the mead-hall with a purposeful expression on his face, which changed rapidly to a mask of dismay as the odor of sweat and old garbage passed his nostrils and entered his lungs.

"Thane-Halls were not kept in a sanitary condition as were modern buildings, since they had no sewage disposal systems, besides which, the inhabitants of mead-halls were generally past the point where they could detect odors of any sort.

"Since Harold was completely unprepared for an emergency regarding perceptions of the olfactory center, he was quite overwhelmed by the range and intensity of sensation resulting from the impressions gathered by the aforementioned nose. In short, Harold fainted from the stink.

"He awakened within a short time, to find himself lying on an animal pelt of some sort. It, too, had a distinct odor — almost as if tanning had not yet been perfected. There were perhaps fifteen people peering down at him.

"He felt as if he were viewing them through a fish-bowl. This created in Harold a feeling of paranoia. Harold had, as a result of his stay in America, become overly suspicious of anyone displaying even the slightest expression

of benevolence or altruism, and these people were definitely
smiling.

"What is the secret of gianthood?" Harold asked with
bravado in spite of his fearful feelings about them.

"They all laughed, and drove him out, believing him to be
possessed by something definitely unpleasant."

CHAPTER SIX

The Companions

"Harold was beginning to recognise that the direct approach might not be too effective. He came to a small clump of trees within which an old woodcutter was chopping wood.

"Pardon me, old chap," he began. "Are you familiar with the secret of gianthood?"

"Only Odin knows the secret of gianthood," the old man replied, "now get lost," he added with a polite smile.

"Had the old man not smiled, Harold would have taken it as an insult. But he had always been taught at the Public School that if someone smiles at one, no matter what they say, one must always be polite in return.

"Harold continued down the road, searching for anyone who could give him even the slightest hint of information about this *Mr. Odin*.

"It was a few hours' march, when he saw a man capering madly down the path. He appeared to Harold as if he had ants in his pants.

"Pardon me," Harold began...

"Can't stop now," the man yelled out. "Got ants in my pants!"

"But this is important..." Harold pleaded.

[29]

"Nothing else is important when you've got ants in your pants!" The man retorted.

"But I simply must locate Mr. Odin," Harold shouted after the man's back. Suddenly the man stopped and turned.

"Say, that *is* important," he said. "Perhaps I can help you after all." And he sat down on the ground, motioning Harold to sit down beside him.

"I thought you had ants in your pants?" Harold solicitously inquired, curious at how the man had mastered his squirming so quickly.

"So I do!" the man exclaimed, jumping up and running off once again. "Perhaps another time!" he shouted over his shoulder.

"Harold realized that reminding the man about his affliction was not what he should have done but the moment was gone beyond recapture.

"And so he continued down the path, until he came to a small village in which he found a fountain. As he sat there pondering the enigma of gianthood, he became aware of a man in a long blue overcoat, walking past. The stranger seemed to recognize him, and he thought he vaguely recognized the stranger, also.

"How can this be?" he asked himself. "I have only recently arrived and could not possibly know this man — and yet, not only do I recognize him, but he also appears to know me from somewhere or other." And risking rebuttal, he asked in a tremulous voice, "Do we know each other?"

"Why, Harold, you old sonofagun!" exclaimed the man in the blue overcoat, "I *thought* it was you, at first, but then I wondered why you hadn't said anything to me when I passed and that caused uncertainty in me."

"Harold was embarrassed about not knowing the man's name. Then, before he knew it, the opportunity to admit it had passed beyond recall.

"Thus he had lost the only way he knew of to discover the identity of this man — direct questioning. As a result,

Harold would be forced to cunningly direct the conversation to the question of identity without admitting that he had no idea who the other man was.

"How did you say you spelled your name?" Harold sounded only mildly interested.

"Same as everyone else does."

. "But it's hard for me to get the letters straight," Harold went grimly on. "I have some difficulty with my spelling," he added.

"So do I, Harold," the other man admitted.

"You don't say," said Harold, his mind whirling with alternatives for another equally tactful approach to the subject.

"Say, Harold, have I ever told you the story of Odin and the pear tree?"

"Can't recall the story, Mr. umph-*um*..." Harold mumbled. "Although, as you probably know, I am most interested in this Mr. Odin, and in particular to know where he can be found."

"Of course you are, Harold, he agreed. We *all* want to know where to find Odin."

"He began telling Harold stories mainly about the sons of Odin — Thor, Loki and the all-seeing Heimdall. He explained that Thor is called 'Thor Odinsson' because he is the son of Odin.

"Excuse me, *hrmph hum um*," Harold interrupted in the middle of a story about how Thor recovered his hammer from the Frost Giants, "but surely you are aware that none of these stories tell me anything about how to go about locating this Mr. Odin."

"You want to find him? You got a better chance to succeed if you understand him enough to be able to guess where he's likely to be. Why do you think I been telling you all these stories about him?"

"Yes, but do you think you can tell me how to find him without so much guesswork?"

"Guesswork? I'm not going to *tell* you! I'm going *with* you! Imagine meeting the old man hisself! Why, ever since I found out about your quest, I thought to myself, 'Irving the Intellect, that ought to be exciting; a quest to find Odin.' I do want to come along...if you'll have me as a companion."

"Uh...of course, *Irving*. I'd like nothing better." Harold's voice weakened from the relief at knowing the man's name and also not unimportantly at having a companion with him who knew the countryside and the local customs...unless he, too, was a time traveler. He wondered momentarily about this, but he knew better than to ask.

"The two of them set off in the general direction of Odin's home — or so Irving thought. Harold found himself continuing to wonder how they seemed to know each other, since they had never met before, but having just been subjected to several hours of 'tales of Odin' in which he had learned little or nothing about Odin, he kept his thoughts to himself.

"By the time they reached the inn, it was late afternoon, and the hostel was crowded with travelers who did not wish to chance the road at night. They were given a room on the lower floor, and prepared to settle in for the night.

"Too bad we didn't get here a little earlier, Harold. We could have had a room on the upper floor."

"Why would we want that?"

"Robbers have a harder time getting into an upper floor window. The lower rooms can be entered too easily."

"But what have we got that anyone would find worth stealing?" Harold asked.

"Quite right, Harold. Hadn't thought of that."

"There was a knock on the door, and Irving bid the person outside to come inside. The door opened, revealing a short fat man in monk's robes. He came into the room, closing the door behind him, and moving with the grace that only a completely sotted fat person can have. His movements reminded Harold of a weather balloon that has been half-deflated and then rolled across a windy field.

"Excuse me," the monk apologized. "I was looking for the men's room." He staggered out once again, muttering disconnected lines from several different well-known limericks.

"I beg your pardon?" inquired Harold, mildly annoyed at the disturbance of his semi-private lodgings.

"Another member of our band," Irving announced. "He likes puns and such, so he's got to be fun to have as a traveling companion," Irving added.

"But he's stinking drunk!" Harold said.

"Aren't we all?" Irving agreed. "But by tomorrow he'll be so sober he won't remember a decent joke."

"The monk had wandered back into the hallway as they spoke, and they heard him bellowing all the way into the common room, where everyone had gathered in order to eat, spread gossip, trade highway robber stories and toss off one-liners.

"You mean he's going to come with us?" asked Harold.

"Oh, he's absolutely essential for the attainment of our quest, Harold."

"You mean he is going to provide the power of prayer and spiritual guidance?"

"No, the Church owns most of the lands we'll be going across. Without him we would be taken as slaves or hanged as freemen."

"Hanged?" Harold anticipated trouble in getting to sleep after that, and so he and Irving got up and went out to the common room in hopes of finding some hot food and a bit of mead, and maybe hear something of Odin's whereabouts.

"As they walked down the hall toward the common room, Irving mentioned that the name of the monk was 'Friar Feel,' and that he, too, had been searching for Odin.

"Harold, oddly enough, was not aware that the name 'Friar Feel' was an obvious name for someone who had been operating primarily from the feeling center, and that the name 'Irving the Intellect' could very well denote that the possessor was someone who had become crystallized in the thinking center, and that they could be understood as analogous representatives of those two brains in humans.''

CHAPTER SEVEN

The Big Secret

"As Harold, Irving and Friar Feel wandered across the countryside in search of Odin, they came upon a man who accosted them from within material similar to the substances in which Harold had once been accustomed to dress himself. That is to say, they encountered someone wearing a suit of armor.

"Good day...Bon jour...Howdy...Gesundheit...Moshi-Moshi!" he began. "My services to you, gentlepersons. I height Sir Stupid, Lord of *Gishdanal.* I have just had a ferocious encounter with a fearsome fire-breathing dragon. What do ye think of *that*?"

"It's all right — don't bother being polite — we're just passing through...we're on our way to find Odin," said Harold, deliberately not saying what he thought of that.

"Odin...you don't say?" said the knight. "Don't mind a little extra company, do ye?"

"Of course not — come along if you've a mind to," offered Friar Feel.

"What is he doing, allowing this character to join us?" Harold whispered to Irving.

"Better let him come," Irving said. "He's one of the

Baron's men. If he took a dislike to us, we'd be in chains."

"Oh."

"Would · have got that dragon, too," the knight complained, "if not for my partner, here. He height 'Hamstrung Heartbeat,' but I call him 'Ham.' He is a passing fair valet, but not of stout great-heart. He is so fearful of being exposed to danger, that he immediately runs away from anything that to him is loud of noise or new of appearance. Thus he gets hurt by tripping over things. In short, he runs like heck."

At this point in his tale The Lord turned away for a moment imparting a deep sigh. "I might add, Gabriel," The Lord said turning toward me once more, "that as a result of his hasty habit of instantaneously displacing his planetary presence from the scene of any potentially dangerous situation this usually resulted in a careless and clumsy compulsive movement at a pace so off-balance that it was impossible to control — thus, he periodically struck solid objects with his own planetary form with not inconsiderable impact.

"In this particular case, he had just gotten his body exceptionally rearranged due to the passive inability of a number of rocks, trees and thorny bushes to move out of his way, in time.

"Ham thought that Odin might be found over at Bush Asgardens, drinking the mead and observing with his well-known appreciative consideration the ladies who occasionally wandered in with whole Italian salamis under their arms. He was, in short, fond of hydroxilated alkane solutions and the company of young females whose psyches had not formed in them any distinction between one male being and another.

"I'm actually glad you decided to come with us," Harold told the knight and his page. "You can show us the ropes, so to speak as they say in America — and interpret for us when we encounter strangers on the road."

"We won't have to interpret," said Ham. "Haven't

you noticed that everyone everywhere speaks English?''

"No, I never took note," admitted Harold.

"Well, we're going in any case, whether we're of use to you or not," said Sir Stupid. "We have our own reasons for going on this adventure," he added.

"Just as you say," said Irving, unwilling to arouse the displeasure of this obviously powerful knight.

"And so, Ham and Sir Stupid set out with the wandering seekers of Odin. Before too long, they came to a ravine, in which they could hear a babbling brook. At the water's edge, they could see a bobcat crouching over the water, staring at the ever-rushing water, baring its teeth in a snarl.

"Stop this babbling. Stop it this instant, do you hear?" the bobcat yelled into the water.

"So...you won't stop babbling...well, we do have *ways* to *make* you stop babbling. Aha! Visitors, I see," he said, rising to greet the newcomers. "Can I be of any help to you?" he said.

"Maybe," said Harold. "Perhaps you can tell us where Odin may be found."

"He might be over to *Utgard*. But he won't talk to anybody little. Never has had anything to do with little folks. *Of course, if you were giant-sized, he'd talk to you for sure.* Excuse me, please," he told them, turning toward the water once again. "Stop it! Stop that babbling!" Finally, frustrated with his efforts to get the brook to cease its babbling, he jumped onto a tree in which a squirrel had been sitting, observing the incident.

"I never heard about Odin not talking to little folks," he said to the bobcat.

"Me neither," the bobcat admitted. "I think I just made it up."

CHAPTER EIGHT

How To Be A Giant

"Harold and his companions had no idea how they were going to ask Odin about *becoming* giants if they had to be giant-sized before he would talk to them! But they were confident that something inexplicable would happen — thus solving the dilemma.

"The most obvious method of attaining gianthood was to ask a giant about it. So they decided to travel together to the land of the giants, called the country of *Ramiq*.

"Along the way, Irving — who knew about all such matters — explained that the land of giants had a population of only a few dozen, as that was the extent of the country's ability to support inhabitants.

"The bravest humans will not dare to live in the country of *Ramiq*," said Irving. "Even though they will inhabit the most loathsome of seaports and filthiest of towns, and infest virtually every part of the world, they have never settled in the land of giants...

"It is perhaps just as well, for if humans had inhabited that country, all the giants would surely by now have completely died off. As it is, the population has remained stable for the past thousand years or more."

"It was then that along came a giant. The ground trembled when he was within half a mile of our heroes. You could not only see him from that distance, but you could smell him, there being a stiff wind behind him and the sun to your back.

"Hey!" Harold shouted into the sky, which was where the giant's head was, although not philosophically — "How does a fellow get to be giant-sized around here?"

"Rather than answer Harold's question through unnecessary chatter, the giant responded with his huge balled-up fist which landed with a thud only a few inches from where Harold stood, waiting for a reply. Harold literally bounced and flew a few feet into the air, and when he came down again, he realized that they must have committed some social blunder.

"They all immediately — as one unit — retired full-speed to the woods to think things over with more care.

"They remained for some time at the edge of the woods and, finally, at nightfall, Irving declared that it was clear as heck that they were going to need some help.

"It is clear as heck," said Irving, "that we are going to need some help."

"Everyone agreed Irving was right, but no one could clearly suggest how they could decide on what kind of help to get."

CHAPTER NINE

The Mysterious Stranger

"After only a few minutes on the road, they came upon a wandering pilgrim dressed in palmer's robes, walking on the dirt ruts as if he were stepping upon rice paper.

"Who are you...where are you going?" the stranger asked.

"We are seekers after Odin," said Irving, "and we are on a journey to find him wherever he may be."

"I shall walk with you a ways," the wandering palmer replied.

"Can you help us locate Odin?" asked Harold.

"Can anyone help anyone else do anything?" the man countered. "How you find Odin depends upon what you make of experiences and impressions gathered by you. This can only be partially assisted by another. You yourself must make the intentional efforts to recognize your experience as it really is in the nonfantastic world."

"After a while they came to a tree, which swayed and creaked, even though there was no wind. The wanderer stopped and approached the tree, standing and listening underneath the branches.

"The tree says that it is in pain; there is something in its side that hurts it. It is asking us to please stop for a while and help it by removing whatever it is, so that it may breathe quietly once again.''

"We haven't time to stop now," Harold said. "We must continue to find Odin. Besides, how can a tree talk?''

"The others agreed with Harold, and all of them began to seriously doubt the sanity of their new companion.

"They continued to walk but, after a half hour, the wanderer suddenly stopped in the middle of the road.

"I thought I smelled honey in that tree," he said. "Maybe there's a hive inside there.''

"Really?" said Irving. "Then let's go back there and get some.''

"Yes," Sir Stupid agreed, "we could eat some now and take the rest to market. That would give us spending money for our journey.''

"Just as you wish," the wanderer said. But when they got back to the tree, a great number of other travelers were already gathering a huge quantity of honey from a hole in the side of the tree.

"We're in luck!" one traveler cried out to the seekers of Odin. "There is enough honey in here to support an entire village! Now we poor travelers can become rich merchants and live in security and peace for the remainder of our lives.''

"And so, Harold and his band of men went on their way again. After a while they came to a very high mountain. On the slope of the mountain near the base they had to stop again, this time because the wanderer thought he heard something in the ground. He stooped down to listen. There was a peculiar humming coming from the earth, and he put his ear closer to the ground.

"I hear millions of tiny ants digging through the dirt below us," he reported. "They have come across some strange stones which are obstructing their progress. They wish us to help them. Shall we stop and give them assistance, or simply continue on our way?''

"The business of insects is not our business," Harold was firm. "Let us continue. I, at any rate, am going to go on, for if we keep stopping in this way, we will never find Odin."

"Stay, if you wish," said Friar Feel, "and grovel around in the dirt. But we are going on with our quest."

"All right, if you all agree to go on, then I won't argue," he said. "But they do say that all beings are connected somehow, and this event may have some connection with our journey together."

"I don't see how," said Irving.

"Not so I can tell," agreed Harold. The others chorused agreement with this, and so they all continued their journey.

"It was when they stopped for the night that Sir Stupid discovered he had lost his knife. Thinking he might have dropped it somewhere near the anthill, which was the only other place they had stopped that day, they waited until daybreak and then went back to the anthill to retrieve it.

"When they got to the anthill there was no knife around, but there were some people — covered with mud — sitting at the side of the road. Next to them was a giant mound of gold coins.

"We have just dug these up from out of that anthill," they explained. "We were walking along the road when a voice called to us, saying, "Dig here for that which is rock to some and gold to others." We did, and now, as you can see, we are rich."

"Ah, if only we had stopped," Harold said. "We would have all the money we needed. Now, as it is, we will have to earn every penny from day to day."

"They continued on their way, until they came to a river where there was a ferry that brought travelers back and forth across the water, and they waited for the ferry to arrive on their side of the river.

"No sooner had they reached the shore, than a large fish rose to the surface, and began to bubble and thrash about.

"The fish is saying he has swallowed a stone," the

wanderer said, "and is asking for our mercy. He wishes us to bring a certain herb for him to eat which will make him cough up the stone and give him peace once again."

"But that was the moment the ferry landed, and since they were impatient to get ahead in their journey, and were also upset at the mistakes they had already made, they pushed each other — and the wanderer as well — onto the raft, and told the ferryman to take them across.

"They slept very soundly that night in a teahouse on the opposite shore. The next morning, as they began to breakfast with tea and cakes provided for them by someone who felt in himself the impulse of charity toward all travelers, the ferryman came in and kissed the hand of the wanderer, thanking him for the luck he brought.

"I was about to leave for home at the usual time," he told them, "when I saw you standing on the opposite bank. I knew that unless I came and brought you over, you would have to spend the night out in the open. So I resolved to make just one more trip across the river, even though I was cold and hungry, and you seemed to be poor and unable to pay for it.

"But afterward, when I was about to put the raft away, I saw a large fish trying to swim ashore in order to eat an herb. All I did was go over to the fish, and bring it to the plant. It ate some of the plant, and then disgorged this..." he said, drawing a huge, flawless and priceless diamond out of his pouch. "And after that, it slipped back into the water again."

"You betrayed us!" Harold shouted at the wanderer. "Our misfortunes have been bad enough, but now we have to know about all the possibilities we will miss in life by not knowing about the treasures to be discovered in the trees, anthills and fish!"

"At that, the wanderer quietly got up from the table and went out the door. They saw him wandering down the road, taking up with yet another traveler who was at that moment explaining to the wanderer the dangers and purposes of his own journey. They walked on, not knowing what to do.''

CHAPTER TEN

A Happy Reunion

"Harold and his companions had been walking all day, and they were tired and hungry when they arrived at a tree that had a sign hammered onto it, about ten feet off the ground. *Yggdrasil*, the sign read, and right next to the tree was a gushing fountain that seemed to bubble right up from the ground.

"After they rested they cooked an afternoon meal of roast chicken and potatoes, and spent the afternoon discussing ideas and swapping anecdotes. As the woods were darkening, and evening came on them, Harold suddenly realized that they had been talking so much that they had completely forgotten about their quest.

"And as he sat there under the fountain, he heard it bubble and gurgle, which said sound inevitably reminded Harold of scenes in his early childhood in which he had been burped.

"And when his passive inner impressions began in this way to influence his planetary body, as is common among humans, he became suddenly very calm, allowing the automatic processes arising in the autonomic nervous system to function without interference from his intellectual and feeling centers for once. That is to say, it assisted his digestion.

"But as cold and clear as the waters of the fountain were, no one dared to drink from it after Harold told them about the experience he had endured on a visit to Mexico City, which resulted in an unique organic effect which forced him to automatically eject the contents of his pre-digesting organ following the ingestion of liquids containing certain very antipathetic microorganisms.

"Suddenly, perhaps as a result of the combination of the said sound-impressions received by his organism originating from the said fountain combined with the arousal of the memory and subjective impressions resulting from the aforementioned 'Montezuma's Revenge', Harold began to recall vividly as if it were just then occurring to him, an incident in which he had gone to Tokyo in order to attend a business convention. It was during this visit to the country of Japan that he became, again as a result of the ingestion of the local water, as is said, 'as sick as a whirling dervish his first time around.'

"And as a result of the said ingestion of inhabited water, along with a negative response to rapidly rising and falling water below the ship, Harold unavoidably manifested the results of his already partially digested dinner on the journey back to the States. However, when he later attempted to re-move the results of the aforementioned illness from the lap of his gray wool pants, he without thinking too clearly grabbed and used a silk kimono bought by him from a merchant who had sworn that it was not the type made for tourists, but the kind the Japanese wore themselves. Through this uncon-scious reflex of his to immediately make the results of the disaster vanish, he inevitably transferred the said results of the disaster from his suit-pants to the surface of the kimono.

"He had intended to present the kimono to his ladyfriend in America in the city Chicago, in order to persuade her to accompany him to a little resort in the Catskills for the weekend. He hoped that as a result of this little gift of his, she might consent — in order to save him further expense — to economize on the hotel accomodations. The results of this escapade he had already anticipated with such force of delight and vivid imagination that had he not ejected the contents of his stomach on the lap of his suit, it would have been ruined in any case.

"She met him at the airport, and he felt compelled to present the kimono to her at that moment. For some reason, however, the anticipated tete-a-tete at the resort in the Catskills somehow did not materialize according to his plans.

"The principle reason for this was that she unavoidably noticed — both through visual and olfactory perceptions — the spot on the kimono, and he, unable even for a moment to refrain from telling her the complete truth about everything, explained what had happened on board the ship. It was extremely fortunate for her that Harold spirited her out of the airport and into a taxicab, because in contemporary civilizations of the planet Earth humans are terrified of wild laughter, and tend to cart away anyone caught laughing, only to deposit them more or less permanently in special hospitals until cured of their sense of humor.

"That was why Harold didn't drink the water, and when he told his story to the others, they didn't either, based on the common belief that 'If it could happen once, it could happen again.'

"What a pity that they did not — due to this prejudice of theirs which connects unrelated earlier experiences to events proceeding in the present — partake of this water of the tree *Yggdrasil*, the Tree of Knowledge.

"Had they done so, they could have easily bypassed all the later efforts they were constrained to make on behalf of their quest for gianthood.

"Of course, on the other hand, had they not made those efforts, the largest draught of such water would have had no effect on them, since only at the last moment is such an 'assisting factor' of any real benefit, as it only amplifies, but does not cause, factors of consciousness already present in the Being.''

CHAPTER ELEVEN

Power — How To Get It And Use It

"As they sat underneath the Tree of Knowledge, they heard someone walking through the underbrush nearby.

"Hi!" shouted Sir Stupid. "Who goes there?"

"An old woman emerged from the woods, and came up to them.

"Just an old woman who is walking back to her house after a long day's work in the field," she told them.

"Old woman, my left ear!" said Irving. "I'll bet she's a sorceress. Make her tell us some Words of Power that will protect us when we go back into the land of the giants!"

"How about it, then?" Harold asked her.

"I know of no such words," she said. "Please let me pass."

"No," said Sir Stupid, catching the fever. "Not until you tell us the Words of Power."

"Do you mean that I cannot go home until I tell you these Words of Power?" the old woman asked.

"Yes, that's right," said Harold.

"Then I will tell you," she said. Of course, she only wished to go home, and knew no such words, but she knew better than to argue with someone's beliefs. "I shall give you three words — Words of Great Power," she told them. "Just by uttering these secret words, you will instantly attain temporary powers beyond anything known in the universe, and you will acquire knowledge beyond anything attainable by ordinary man," she continued, having heard a learned scholar speak in this exact manner some years before.

"But you must not use these words unless you are in mortal danger!" she admonished. "For they can become useless if repeated too often!" She told them that because she did not want them to try them out until she was well out of the way. The men could hardly contain their impatience to receive their very own Words of Power.

"Come forward and receive your Words of Power!" she intoned. Of course, she did not know any Words of Power, but she did know a few words in *Marmin*, the secret language spoken only by the giants, which humans were not supposed to know.

"They each came forward — except Sir Stupid and Ham, who considered themselves not worthy to receive such power.

"To Harold, she gave the giant's word meaning 'We.' And to Irving, she gave the word that means 'Were Not.' Finally, to Friar Feel she gave the word in *Marmin* which translated into English means 'Happy.' They, not understanding the words, were satisfied, and she dashed off as quickly as she could.

"They immediately set off for the land of the giants, in order to test their words and through the use of their powers to force a giant to divulge the secret of gianthood.

"This will save us the trouble of having to build a fake giant," Harold said.

"Yes," agreed Irving. "Lucky for us I perceived that she was a sorceress, eh?"

CHAPTER TWELVE

In The Dungeon

"When they arrived in the land of the giants, they were surprised to encounter the carcass of a dead giant, lying by the side of the road. Before they could leave the scene, however, several giants strode over the hill and were upon them.

"*Who killed this countryman of ours?*" the bigger of the two giants demanded.

Harold, believing that his Word of Power would freeze them into statues, shouted his Word at them: "*We!*"

"Of course, the giants understood this word spoken in their own secret language, and therefore took them prisoner. They were brought to the castle of the Prince of Giants, who accused them of murder.

"You were discovered standing over the body, and you admitted the crime!" he shouted at them.

"*Were Not!*" Shouted Irving expecting the walls to shatter, allowing them to walk away in freedom.

"Well, you are obviously lying," the giant Prince said to them, now very angry. "How would you feel if someone killed you?"

"*Happy!*" shouted Friar Feel, trying out his Word of Power.

"You humans are monsters and demons!" shouted the Prince. "What was your motive for killing him?"

"*We were not happy!*" they all cried out at once, believing that escape might require all of their Words of Power.

"You are obviously cold-blooded murderers!" the giant yelled in rage. "Put them in the dungeon and tomorrow morning hang them, as they deserve!"

"They were chained together, and half-dragged across the stone floor, down into the darkness, stumbling and falling against the cold wet walls.

"They came to a narrow passage in which they could see tiny cells, from which hollow-eyed inhabitants stared out at the new arrivals.

"The giant who had dragged them down there thundered through the stinking atmosphere: "Guard!"

"There came a snuffling sound from the other end of the hallway, and a horrible scaly creature emerged from a niche in the stone wall.

"Here's a few more for you."

"Yes, Lord."

"Put them in an empty cell."

"The guard stripped them of their garments so they could not hang themselves, and locked them into the cell. They huddled against the side walls, trying to avoid contact with the heap of garbage near the rear wall.

"Well, what are we going to do now?" Harold asked, looking around for somewhere else to sit except the one item of furniture in the cell — a wooden bucket, the purpose of which was plain to see and to smell.

"I don't know," said Irving. "The Words of Power didn't work."

"Perhaps it is because there is an enchantment on this castle," suggested the friar.

"It's because they weren't Words of Power," Harold snapped. "That was no sorceress. She was just an ordinary old woman."

"Harold, how can you say that?" said Sir Stupid. "She gave you words, didn't she?"

"Yes, but they didn't do anything."

"But she *did admit* that they were Words of Power?"

"That is what she told us," Harold answered.

"Well, then!" said Sir Stupid, "That proves it, doesn't it?"

"It's just that there is a counterspell here," said the friar. "When we discover its formula, we can use our Words of Power to get out of here."

"They heard the sound of dripping water and occasionally a clanking chain would ring out in the darkness.

"Suddenly they noticed a figure approaching them. It seemed to come through the solid rock walls.

"Come with me," the figure spoke to them. They followed it through the walls of the dungeon. They were led to a place where everyone cried out in pain and suffering.

"Who are these people, and where have you taken us?" asked Harold.

"These are people who have failed in their search for Odin, and accepted others in his place," they were told.

"Then they were taken to a place in which everyone was joyful and content, where everyone they saw had beautiful faces and forms.

"Who are they, and where are we now?" asked Friar Feel.

"These are the *bon-ton* people, who chose to follow the way of pleasure."

"But why are they so happy?" asked Sir Stupid.

"They chose pleasure instead of truth," they were told. "Just as those you saw first chose suffering instead of pleasure or truth."

"But isn't happiness what we're after?" asked Harold.

"He who has the truth may choose any mood he wishes to create within himself. But man cannot create truth. He pretends that truth and happiness are one and the same, because happiness is easier to achieve, while it requires great effort and intentional suffering of a very special kind to attain truth. Both happiness and suffering are prisons into which anyone too weak to transcend them is thrown.''

"Suddenly they found themselves in the prison cell once again.

"I will grant you one wish — one *real wish* —'' the guide told them.

"Then I wish to know why we have failed in our common aim,'' said Harold. "And if possible how we can succeed in it.''

"You have almost wasted your lives,'' the guide said.

"Yes, but we've come this far, and you came to help us.''

"You have received my help only because you wished for truth for its own sake and not for your personal gratification — and even then only for a single moment. It was that single moment of real yearning that made me respond to your call for help.''

"The guide began to walk away before Harold and the others could stop him or say anything to this.

"Wait!'' Harold called out.

"You may not come with me,'' said the man. "I must now return to the ordinary world, and so must you. In the world of humans is where your work now awaits you, and that is where you shall go.''

"But when they looked around, they realized that they were no longer standing in the prison cell in the giant's castle, but in an enclosed garden. They walked outside to find themselves once more near the little village at which they had started their quest. Somehow through sheer luck, the traveling seekers after Odin had escaped certain death.''

CHAPTER THIRTEEN

How Humans Think
And Why They Go Mad

"But Lord," I objected, after He had stopped talking. "I cannot yet understand why they could not see clearly where they had been all that time. Why did they believe themselves to be in prison when they were standing in the walled garden? Why didn't they recognize the guide?"

"There are several definite reasons for this, Gabriel. They believe themselves to possess an organ capable of original thought — when in fact it is no more than a simple muscle which happens to contract in a slight spasm whenever a thought arises from the Akashic Archives and passes through it on its way toward the lower vibration cosmoses.

"Thus the resulting after-image of a thought is trapped and held in place for a few moments, giving humans the impression that it originated within their minds — thanks to their puffed up idea of themselves and their imaginary personal powers.

"Just because a trapped thought triggers an involuntary procession of similar but unrelated thoughts and images, humans have the subjective impression that those thoughts came into being because they personally created them 'for the first time ever'.

"But of course, since humans are unable to create original thoughts, and cannot arouse intentionally specific emotions or sensations in themselves through their own will, they cannot begin to even lay a foundation for active consciousness.

"In short, humans ordinarily are forced to allow the passive flow of thoughts coming to them from the *Cathode-Source-Of-All-Thoughts* to lodge in the upper cranial muscle, thus stimulating the mind — which is separate from the organism, but part of the being — to note with varying degrees of attention those thoughts which are being triggered into recall as a result of the primary perceptions and thoughts proceeding from external or higher sources. Thus it was that humans on the planet Earth came to believe that because they are subject to the influences of random thought in an equally random reaction-pattern, they 'obviously and demonstrably' have the ability to think.

"Incidentally, this cranial muscle of theirs serves as the *Anode-Collector* of thoughts proceeding from the source of all thoughts, which are released in bursts of 79,000 at any given moment. But out of the totality of these, the human cranial muscle is only capable of focusing attention on one of them in any given moment. And that single thought of which a human can be aware is suggested at random by the chain-reaction within the third brain as these said bursts of thought pass through it.

"There are, then, no real thoughts or memories belonging to humans, as they would so desperately like to believe.

"This continuous pulsation of bursts of seventy-nine thousand thoughts per moment of time — which incidentally equals One Eternity — provides the basis for the conceptualization of action and existence in any reality anywhere. But as usual, the 'self-limiting factor' in humans makes it possible for them to only become aware of seven of these seventy-nine thousand possible thoughts, which said seven thoughts make up the entire range of their subjective and objective reality.

"And as these thoughts cause spasmodic reactions in the cranial muscle, the cranial muscle serves in its turn as the *Cathode-Source-Of-Emanations* for the sensing center of the human organism, which is a muscle located at the base of their spines.

"In turn, the spasmodic reaction of the Sensing Muscle located in the base of the spine causes the impression — when associated with the thoughts momentarily captured in the cranial muscle at the top of the spine — of *emotions*, which are in reality sensations automatically linked at random with images of various *states of feelings*, but which are actually *states of sensations.*

"For instance, if they have the sensation of tightening of the stomach muscle, shortened breath, and visual oscillation, they call that the sensation *hunger.* But if the same group of sensations is accidentally connected with the thought or image of something threatening, they call it the emotion *fear.*

"In short, they believe that each group of sensations linked with thoughts and images has some deeper meaning and significance, which they call *emotions.*

"Of course, all this has led to the belief, now firmly rooted in them, that they not only have the ability to think and to feel, but that they have another 'something' more spiritual, called by them *instinct*, thanks to which they are able to discern the truth or falsity about anything at all, even those things about which they know absolutely nothing.

"This *instinct* of theirs is, of course, no more objective than an expression of their wish to believe something about themselves...But if one says that to their faces...

"In spite of all these wonderful powers of theirs, if a problem does happen to come along that they cannot solve with these automatically-possessed-at-birth-gifts of theirs — *thinking, feeling,* and *intuition* — they collapse utterly into a mass of protoplasm, due to the simultaneous destruction — only momentarily, however — of their self-esteem and belief in the powers of the thinking, feeling and instinctive centers they imagine themselves to possess.

"And the loss in them of the sustaining force of *Confidence-In-Their-Own-Ability-Through-The-Power-Of-Self-Conceit* in turn produces stress upon the organism leaving them in a natural Essence-state, which is called by their doctors and learned beings knowing everything about human beings — which learned beings call themselves *psychologists* and *psychiatrists* — the state of *neurosis*, and in severe cases of disability, the state of *psychosis*.

"And not only do the said doctors fear the state of natural Essence, but they treat it with what are called *mental health procedures*, such as *chemotherapy*, which sedates the person and makes him unable to exist in a natural Essence state, and *shock therapy* which — since by law he cannot be peeled, cooked and eaten — makes him even more useless than a vegetable.

"And instead of teaching the individual while in the natural Essence state how to operate effectively in the world and *remain* in the Essence state through the positive action of continual stress, these 'persons of the medicinal persuasion' deliberately remove the source of stress and after making sure the person is rendered completely incapable of anything but slow movements and slurred speech, they force the victim, called by them *the patient*, although I would not be, if they tried to do that to me — to focus on early childhood experiences, of course, limiting the incidents to only those which would reinforce their existing beliefs regarding Case Histories As Outlined by the Particular Progenitor of Their Own Brand of Treatment for Severe States of Natural Essence Existence.

"That is, in some cases, all their patients have problems of sibling rivalry, while for other doctors, the patients have had only sexual problems, or only learning problems, and so forth.

"This provides the said doctors with some amusement while waiting for the patient to go mad, due to the ingestion of chemical medications which have the effect of making them *seem* insane whether they are or not.

"You must admit, Gabriel, that this is a good method of ridding themselves of imaginative — and therefore dangerous — individuals who have somehow stumbled onto perceptions of the Real World.

"Ah, Lord, I begin to understand something about these humans. The radical effects of the perception of the Real World would force them to reconstruct their relationships with each other and with the planet. It would, in fact, totally destroy the existing culture and replace it with an ethical one."

"Yes, exactly. And the economics of that change would be a disaster to the power-possessing minority, Gabriel."

"I see."

"Aren't you getting hungry?" He asked, moving toward the serving dishes once again.

"Please, Lord — don't leave me in suspense," I quickly interposed. "What happened to Harold and his companions?"

"Oh, yes...the story...I'd almost forgotten.

"Although they had all agreed previously that in order to meet Odin they would have to seem to be giants, and that the obvious way to accomplish this would be to build a fake giant, wheel it up to a real giant, and ask the secret of gianthood — a giant wouldn't withhold secret information from another giant — they by now realized that none of them knew how to build a fake giant but that they were forced to carry out this plan anyway, as they had exausted all other alternatives known to them..."

CHAPTER FOURTEEN

The Turning Point

"As they walked, Ham suddenly became discouraged. He ran off into the woods, shrieking that nothing was getting accomplished and that they would never be able to build a fake giant that worked. Harold realized that he was right — none of them knew how to make a giant-sized machine operate as if it were a real giant. Without that ability, they were not going to be able to fool a real giant into revealing the secret of gianthood.

"Sir Stupid ran after his long-time friend Hamstrung, but he couldn't run fast enough to catch up to him.

"Then, just as suddenly and without warning, Friar Feel pontifically declared that since the search for Odin was impossible, only a drink of mead could sooth him — and moreover, to calm him from this saddening idea it would require several kegs of mead. He thereupon made his way to the village tavern, and what with his sporadic alternate fits of laughing and crying, interspersed with frequent visits to the men's room, the remaining companions did not get much done in the way of planning.

"After a while, Irving, Sir Stupid and Harold were all precisely as unable to remain vertical as the good monk.

"They simply waited at the tavern until Hamstrung returned. He came trudging toward them only a half-hour later. The reason for this was that Harold had been the first person to come along who had told Hamstrung exactly what to do from minute to minute."

"These humans certainly do have odd ideas, Lord," I said.

"They have an idea even stranger than the impulse of Desire To Be Given Instructions."

"Really, Lord?" I asked. "What is it?"

"It is called the *Impulse of Paranoia.* Archangel Lefkowitz believes this term to be philologically related to the human term which he thinks they use for *extreme anxiety* — the word *clap*. Personally, I do not believe the two terms are related at all. I think the phrase *The Clap* is a term of endearment to a loved one — I have heard it used more than once in a love-relationship. I do not see how this reasoning can be refuted. But back to my story...

"Harold and his companions walked Hamstrung back to the village, and as they did, they discussed plans for the fake giant.

"It has to be fifty feet tall, or forget it," said Harold.

"I just thought of someone who could help us complete our giant," Irving said. "There is a guy name of Moving Hood. He is just the kind of person who could put something like this together."

"So they sent out to the village tavern for more sandwiches and skins of mead, and wrapping their take-out lunches in a checkered cloth, they jumped into an ox-cart and clattered off amid laughter and merriment to find Moving Hood. They enlisted him in their project, and returned to the land of giants — this time remaining near the border of the country, well out of sight of any passing giants, in the woods of a neighboring land, called *Penumbria*."

CHAPTER FIFTEEN

Building The Fake Giant

"Moving Hood was a great deal of help in getting the fake giant to work — now, finally it was engineered very well indeed. But they still needed some method of control. Up to this point, they had constructed an apparatus that was capable of bending, walking, running — and even hopping. But there was no central system for controlling the giant.

"As it was, everyone had to be in different parts of the giant, in order to pull levers, push rods, turn the pulley-wheels and work the guy-ropes. Orders had to be shouted from the top of the giant down to the others below. When the shouting began, one could hear the general racket from miles away.

"This won't do," said Harold. "What we need is a centralized control system that can be operated by one person."

"Moving Hood said that he knew a person named Sacrilege LeDesirous who could develop such a system, but that he did not think LeDesirous would agree to take part in their adventure, because he was unlikely to leave his bed.

"Why?" asked Friar Feel.

"Because there is nearly always someone else in it with him," said Moving Hood.

"Harold and Irving decided to go to see him anyway, and try to persuade him to join their quest. And just as Moving Hood had predicted, LeDesirous was in bed, in this instance with a young nun who had become aroused during confession and needed a 'little something' to get her through the next few prayer meetings.

"Harold and Irving explained to LeDesirous that if he helped them develop a central control system for their fake giant, he could have the giant when they were finished with it.

"What good would a fake giant be to me?" he wanted to know.

"You ever go to bed with a giant female?" asked Irving, slyly.

"What a time we'd have!" he said. Of course, had he ever *seen* a giant woman, he would never have joined the project.

"When they had completed the giant, they wheeled it up to a real giant. But as they had forgotten to add a voice to the fake giant, the real giant became curious.

"Why doncha talk?" the giant asked. The fake giant just stood there.

"Hey, whatsa matta witcha, huh?" the giant demanded. "Cat gotcher tongue?" The fake giant just stood there, and he don't say *nuthin.*

"Aw, youse ain't no fun," the real giant complained, glowering in rage. He balled up his fist, slamming it down on the fake giant's head.

"They waited until the giant stomped angrily off before rolling the fake giant back into the woods. It was fortunate for them that giants do not live up to their name in the matter of perception, awareness and intelligence.

"Up to the time of the aforementioned disaster occurring to the fake giant, Harold had not concerned himself with the workings of its internal parts. But now he realized it was imperative to perfect the fake giant's motive controls, altering those things that did not work effectively. He did not want to repeat the last experiment — especially with himself standing in the vulnerable head part of the fake giant.

"So he asked Moving Hood to go through the giant body with him, and explain the various parts of the fake giant — which they had named 'Morris'.

"They began their tour in the propulsion room. Harold was very impressed with the number of gears and levers.

"Most of these gears don't do anything," Moving Hood said. "I just got carried away with whittling."

"Oh."

"It is mostly a matter of working the energy spenders and suppliers in unison. You will note that this little thingamabob here has a sliding door on it," he added.

"Harold bent down to get a closer look at it. There was a pattern of very ornate and intricate detail engraved into it. Around the sides of the door a number of glass tubes ran into and out of the box surrounding the door. Most of them went into an overhead compartment of some sort, that had a rounded bottom and drew almost to a point at the top, looking very much like a huge copper teardrop.

"How does it work?" asked Harold.

"Never mind how it *works*! You should ask what it *does*!" replied Moving Hood.

"What does it do?" Harold obliged.

"This is the propelling mechanism of the whole apparatus," explaining Moving Hood. "Without this, the giant would have no power in any of its separate parts."

"But how *does* it work?" Harold insisted.

"It is very complicated."

"Make the attempt anyway to explain it to me," Harold prompted.

"All right. There are, as you are already aware, three basic forces in the universe; motion, stillness, and endlessness. And all three unique forces must be employed in order to make movement of any sort possible. If we want to get an object to move, we can alter the amount and direction of the flow and interaction of their vivifying forces, right?"

"Harold did not know, so he agreed with him in order not to appear ignorant to his companions.

"Moving Hood opened the little sliding door, to reveal within the device a great number of dyed gut and hair strings in varying widths and lengths. "Each string is colored according to the number of vibrations it emits per second when plucked." Harold twanged one, to see what would happen.

"Don't do that!" yelled Moving Hood, too late. The giant lurched in its scaffolding, almost toppling over backwards.

"Good grief!" exclaimed Harold. "Do you mean to say that a little string like that can have that powerful an effect?"

"Of course it can! Each string is amplified by a resonator, making the effect of any vibration a thousand times more powerful. The moving parts of the giant are all run by such vibrations. Each string does something different to the moving parts — but if we pluck them in chordal arrangements we get combined effects that no number of single strings plucked individually would be able to produce."

"What is this huge lever here for?" Harold asked, indicating a wooden lever that went across the entire upper area of the moving center.

"That," intoned Moving Hood, "is the motivator for the fake giant's penis."

"Penis? What does a fake giant need with a penis?" Harold demanded.

"LeDesirous wouldn't come along unless we put in a penis," Moving Hood told him.

"How does it work?"

"This little lever here extends it," said Moving Hood, "and that giant lever overhead moves it up and down."

"Fascinating. Mind if I try it?" asked Harold.

"My cookies are burning!" exclaimed Moving Hood, sniffing the smoky air. He ran into the fake giant's kitchenette, leaving Harold to play with the levers.

"After a few minutes of manipulating the fake giant's penis — which he could not see from that section of the giant, anyway — he got bored and climbed up the ladder into the Operations Room which was Friar Feel's domain.

"Harold discovered the good monk collapsed over a huge mound of copper tubing, which had been fashioned into a vast and intricate design of interconnected coils.

"What's wrong Friar?" asked Harold, when he heard the sobbing emanating from the monk's direction. "Is something the matter with the environmental sensing device?" Concerned about the equipment, Harold leaned over the copper coils in order to examine it for damage.

"Hey, get off the wet-bar!" yelled the monk, stifling his sobbing for the moment.

"*What* wet bar?" Harold asked in surprise. "I don't see any wet bar! All there is in this room is this sensing-device you made for the giant."

"Sensing Device? There's the wet-bar!" He said, indicating the mass of copper tubing.

"You mean you built a wet-bar out of the materials you were supposed to use for the construction of an environmental sensing mechanism?" Harold roared as softly as he could, not wishing to appear uptight.

"It is for a very sound and sufficient reason," explained the holy man. "In the event that another giant smashes this model as happened with the previous one, I will have enough juice in me to go limp when the cave-in occurs, thus bearing no harm to my body."

"Harold thought that the good friar had enough padding to make such a precaution superfluous, but he did not wish to offend him and so, biting back any further outburst, he stomped up the ladder into the fake giant's head, where most of the control and perceiving apparatus had been located.

"He was even more astounded by the array of apparatus in

the head than he had been with the gears and pully systems in the abdomen. It seemed to him that Aristarchos of Samos, Leonardo DaVinci, Rube Goldberg and Archimedes had all conspired to compound as infinitely complex a mechanism as possible.

"What is it?" he asked Irving, who had been under the console making a few adjustments.

"It could be described as a *Cacophonic Utilizer Of The Primary Triad Of Forces According To Scale Derived By Natural Function Of The Seven Steps Of Activity Through Interaction With The Three Steps Of Passivity By The Intermediary Of A Catalytic Agent Naturally Existing In Space And Time.*

"What is the catalytic agent?" asked Harold.

"Why, *we* are," Irving said.

"How does it work?" That incredible complex contraption began to arouse in Harold the beginning impulses of a condition which could be described as *vague feelings of inferiority brought about by only partially recognized self-observations of the overwhelming effects resulting from a sudden confrontation with the apparent complexity of an apparatus of unknown properties.*

"In short, he felt the desire to scream non-stop for several minutes, but refrained from doing so for social reasons.

"Irving smirked in a brotherly grin, when he realized how confused Harold was about all this.

"This instrument right here is called a *Khodoril*. It prevents undesirable interactions from occurring. And then there is a *hnots*, which stores up energy for the time that it will be required. It all functions on the basis of the usual variations occurring on this planet in conformity with the Law of Trinity moving through the octave in accordance with the Law of Ninefoldness."

"The what?" Harold asked.

"Law of Ninefoldness. Surely you know the geometry which creates the Law of Ninefoldness."

"No, haven't heard a thing about it before now," said Harold.

"Well, it simply means that any emanation of a tone has a finite number of dynamic interactions with other tones, producing a known number of harmonic radiations, which can be predicted on a definite expanding scale and position in relation to that scale, and that...oh, of course — you're just joking with me! Everyone, even the most churlish of lads, knows about the Law of Ninefoldness!"

"Yes, that's it; I'm just fooling," Harold quickly agreed, wishing at all costs to avoid having to live with the name 'Foolish Harold.'

"Harold began to think once again about the scene that he had witnessed on the old hag's crystal ball. *It's all very well to build a fake giant*, he thought, *but what about me becoming giant-size? That's a completely different matter...* A few moments later, he realized that he must have missed something Irving was saying.

"...which hooks up directly with the *Hvarnookarnian relay system*, thus eliminating the carbon process by re-routing the positive pitch alternately into the hydrogen screen, taking the material vibration up so that it can be refined through the *Uzqinutiunard machine* until it formulates at the *permanent 24* level."

"Of course," Harold said, "That's obvious."

"Now then, since we can predetermine the effect of the increased size of the giant body by the Law known as *The Increase Of Internal Inertia Not Only According To Weight And Size, But Also There Is Of Course A Certain Amount Of Loss Caused By The Structural Difference Between A Human Body And A Giant Body Under Ordinary Conditions Except That If We Want The Giant Body To Look Like A Real Giant We Do Not Alter The External Design To Accomodate Internal Mechanical And Energy Transfer Stress Factors Because If We Did That It Would Look Funny So We Have To Synthesize Internal Moving Parts To Account For The*

Variation Between The Way Both Types Of Bodies React To Gravity And Motion."

"That's the *name* of the Law?" asked Harold, incredulously.

"Yes. It gets worse if I try to explain it," said Irving.

"Now, with the help of devices like this..." he indicated a long row of glass tubes of obviously ersatz manufacture, built to tolerances of an inch in any given direction, "...these tubes are evacuated of all gases — a task supposedly impossible, and made even more difficult by the fact that M. Boyle has not yet existed. The device which was used for that was the only item not invented by the Greeks, and so it was necessary to develop it ourselves. It is an obscure application of the *Law of Agriventakiolno*, or the *Law Of The Results Of Interactions Occurring When Wet Objects Slide Across Slippery Surfaces."*

"Wait a moment, Lord," I interrupted. "I can see that the internal structure of the fake giant's body has to be altered to accomodate the increase in size and lack of internal musculature. But I do not understand how the *Law of Agriventakiolno* applies to the problem."

"It is not obvious in this case, it is true, Gabriel. Perhaps I can illustrate its use by giving you an example of another time it was used, this time by myself, to determine the facts in an otherwise completely unverifiable set of data."

CHAPTER SIXTEEN

The Law Of Agriventakiolno

"It was in the matter of the seemingly endless string of self-perpetuating ignorances fostered among humans for their own amusement, which is called by them *science*.

"There are among these humans certain singular properties, which when viewed impartially from above are objectively bizarre. They deliberately terrify themselves with self-manufactured ideas, which are imaginary laws of nature of course not corresponding at all to genuine laws proceeding in the universe — and who should know better about that than *me?*

"One of these sciences of theirs, called *spiritism*, expresses the belief — along with numberless *facts* and theories — that there is somehow something more dead than humans, called *ghosts*.

"This is obviously a way of fantasizing that humans of the planet Earth — not to mention the entire cosmos — are 'solid', and that these ghosts are in relation to this solidness less solid than they are. It is upon this assumption, that the Earth is solid matter having solid objects within it, that still more fantastic sciences of theirs are based, including such absurd topics of study as *physics, chemistry, medicine,* and *astronomy,* among other still more fantastic sciences, based upon even more outlandish beliefs.''

"Like what, Lord?"

"Take their science of *astrology,* for instance...No, on the other hand, I had better not say anything. Should any of this get back to them...It's all right to make derisive comments about their physics, chemistry, medicine and astronomy, even to call them 'hairless rats'...But let someone say even the slightest thing about their science of astrology, and...Gabriel! Forget that I even mentioned it!

"These sciences of theirs are a collection of theories and proofs relating to beliefs about the world and about themselves. As our beloved Archangel Lefkowitz says: 'If they cannot understand something, through these wonderful sciences of theirs, they can at least explain it.'

"But, let's see, now..." He continued in an absent-minded way. "We left Harold examining the workings of the fake giant Morris..."

"Lord," I said. "That is a crummy stunt. Come on, tell me about the Law of Agriventakiolno, and how you applied it for the purpose of elucidating something you wanted to find out.''

"All right," he agreed. "I had heard that there was a 'ghost-hunter' operating in the city of Chicago, in America. Ghost hunters of this type were called 'mediums'. I wanted to find out if it was true that she was a 'medium', and so I traveled there personally. It was necessary for me to do this, as I could not trust the impartiality and objectivity of another individual's report on this vital subject.

"When I got there, I went to the abode of the lady reported to be a medium. Immediately and without hesitation, with her cooperation, of course, I applied the *Law of Agriventaki-olno* in order to personally elucidate for myself the answer to this burning question.''

"And?" I asked. "Was she a medium?"

"No..." He said. "It turned out she was a 'large'...Now can I continue with my story?"

CHAPTER SEVENTEEN

Empty Bags With
Walls Of Skin

"Of course," I said with that tone usually reserved for reactions to puns.

"...Harold continued to plague Irving with questions about the construction of the fake giant. He was particularly interested in a contraption which Irving described as *Actualizer For The Sacred Combination Of Liashko*, or 'the-correlation-of-quiet-moments-of-the-operation-of-the-machine-with-moments-of-direct-personal-perception-of-the-deep-self-for-the-purpose-of-formulating-and-performing-a-specific-action.''

"However, just at that moment, a mob composed of local peasants carrying an assortment of what are called 'deadly instruments for the creation of mayhem' emerged from the woods into the clearing where Harold and his companions had been constructing the fake giant.

"What are you going to do?'' yelled Sir Stupid, who had been standing guard at the base of the scaffolding.

"We're gonna tear that thing down!'' snarled the leader of the mob.

"But it's just a mechanical giant that we're going to use to find out the secret of gianthood,'' explained the knight.

"We don't care what it is, or what it's for!" screamed one of the vigilantes in fear.

"But it's perfectly harmless, and we aren't doing anything to bother you," Sir Stupid reasoned.

"It don't matter what *you* think," the mob leader asserted. "If it's big, it's *bound* to be dangerous!"

"Excuse me, Lord," I interrupted. "I don't want you to consider me a super-idiot, but I have not understood a word you said since you began to explain the Law of Agriventakiolno. Is there something wrong with me, or what?"

"This little problem of yours was not unexpected. It has arisen because you have not allowed your consciousness to conform to the Law *Umbarzalmishkoswarmy — Accept Your Impressions On The Most Obvious Level First, Before You Take It Anywhere Else.*"

"Ohhh..." I said. "Then you mean she really *was* a 'large'!"

"*Now* may I continue my story?" He asked. "So, as I was saying, the local peasants were crawling out of the woods, in order to completely destroy the fake giant being assembled there."

"Excuse me again, Lord," I said.

"What is it?"

"It has just occurred to me, Lord, that in the manufacture of the fake giant, although very definite steps were taken to assure the proper motive and arresting forces, and the correct counter-balance factors were incorporated also into the design, no actual representation of the internal organs we hear so much about regarding these humans of the planet Earth had been made."

"That is true, Gabriel. As the humans of the planet Earth would say, that fake giant just had no guts."

"Yes, but, Lord, in the explanation of the workings of the fake giant 'Morris' that you have reported to me, it was impossible not to notice that the interior of the fake giant does not even correspond to any of these, but to other internal parts, instead. Where is the substitute for the stomach, and the intestines? And especially, where is the substitute for the heart, about which we hear so much from these humans, and which they consider so important.''

The Lord nodded his head in agreement. ''You are right, Gabriel. It pleases me that you have noticed this, as it shows that you are paying attention to seemingly unimportant — but actually vital — details.

''There is no relation between the internal organization of the fake giant Morris and the internal organs of the humans of the planet Earth, because there *are* no internal organs in the humans existing on the planet Earth! That is, under normal — for them — conditions of existence, there aren't.

''The beings of the medical profession on the Continent Atlantis knew — as does any being of objective reason — that humans are actually nothing more than bags of hot air with walls of skin, whose whole purpose in life consists of taking air coming from the larger cosmos into their bags and exhaling it after having warmed it up. But they have ruined this purpose by adding to the warmed-up air certain vocal vibrations, called by them 'speech'.

''They knew that anything found inside the body was not an ordinary inhabitant, but a visitor from another world.

''These Atlantean physicians had at that time the knowledge with which to help those unfortunate humans afflicted with interior parasites to rid themselves of them. These ancient medical techniques for clearing out the body were called *Girginaqirmetod*, which translates into our language as *exorcism*.

''Humans today are fearful of anything coming to them from ancient times — so much so that they not only refuse to allow others to practice these techniques, but hold superstitious beliefs regarding them to the extent that they treat anyone interested in such subjects in much the same way as they invariably treat my special messengers.

"This modern ignorance about the true causes of what humans call *bacterial and viral infections, sepsis* and improper psychical organizations called *paranoia, schizophrenia, dementia praecox*, and *the blues* is a direct cause of the improper training of the modern-day physicians.

"Even more importantly, modern physicians have been misled by a physician of their Sixteenth Century, who made experiments that have served to hopelessly confuse the medical profession for over four hundred years.

"This physician named Vesalius, tried to reconstruct medical knowledge after the disappearance of the Continent Atlantis and the subsequent loss of all real medical knowledge.

"His experimentation, which was prompted by the failure of an earlier physician named Galen to correctly map and interpret the human body, was in the subject of human anatomy, specifically the field of 'chirurgie', called in modern times 'surgery'.

"This required the opening of the outer bag, called the 'skin', along with cutting and prying into the contents — if any — of the said bag of skin. Medical beings today are so fascinated with the idea of cutting into and opening bags that they have conveniently overlooked the fact that the various items they find inside are totally alien to the body.

"Instead of performing their proper medical office, which would be to rid the body of these infestations that have accidentally lodged within the body, they try with all their cunning and ingenuity to invent purposes for the existence of parasitic inhabitants of the body, and perform all sorts of strange experiments with them.

"For so long have they done this, that they have actually begun to believe that these interior parasites are a natural part of the human body, calling them by names which suggest that they have always been parts of the human body.

"After the disappearance of the Continent Atlantis, none of the former residents managed to escape, as you already know.

"Nevertheless, a few elements of real medicine managed somehow to survive with minor alterations.

"When a plague arose in the country of *Ashikhark*, the physicians recognized an invasion of internal parasites, and began — although not with the skill and knowledge of the Atlantean physicians — to draw these interior parasites out of the bodies of afflicted persons, depositing the said parasites into *canopic jars* for proper disposition according to the *humors* of each parasite.

"The ordinary inhabitants, not understanding Objective Medicine, directed that the physicians cut into the body and actually remove the afflicted parts. Before this, they had removed the parasites only through the process of, as I have already mentioned, *exorcism*.

"Due to the new practice of cutting into the bag, the practice of real medicine failed to develop once again on the planet Earth. Later generations continued to perform this "canopic jar operation", but in a crude manner by cutting the bag open after its death — but before corruption had set in — and preserving the interior parasites found within the bag, in order that the deceased could exhibit them in the afterlife, demonstrating exactly what had caused the death.

"It is strange to me, Gabriel, that such individuals who know the real methods of Objective Medicine — such as my most recent Son, who became known there as a *Nazorean*, or healer — are invariably run out of town on a rail, while those who do not understand real medicine, and have an urgent craze to cut bags wide open, are allowed to freely cut bodies open and fish around in there, looking for 'who knows what'.

"After they have probed and cut the various parasites they find inside, their curiosity about them satisfied, they once again sew up the bag — *leaving those parasites in there* — and moreover, leaving them in such a throbbing condition that even if an attempt to exorcise them were performed later, they would be in no condition to return to their native worlds.

"Vesalius was the first of their physicians to make an effort to catalog these interior parasites, although he had the same unfortunate urge to cut the bag, thus misleading him into believing that these were natural parts of the human body.

"His experiments in the cutting of the bag and subsequent cataloging of parasites led him to several conclusions:

"Whenever one cuts into the bag, there are always present millions of tiny red spheres. And rather than recognizing that they were, as Objective Medicine already knows, *Little Red Pain-Eaters*, he decided — since he could not conceive of inter-dimensional travel, and had no way of knowing that these little beings had individual consciousness — that they had always been present in the body. According to this idea, he decided to call these creatures from the world *Babagan* by a name which suggested that they belonged permanently to the body. He decided that these tiny creatures were a 'homogeneous blob of stuff', which he named *blood*.

"During further probing, he discovered the beings which originated on the planet *Arshav*, which said tube-like creatures are formed similar to what is called on Earth a *racetrack*, who like to race particles of food through themselves and wager between themselves about which particles will finish first — and without which parasites the food ingested by humans would, as is proper to their beings, emerge within moments after ingestion, having already provided the impressions and shocks necessary to the being — and Vesalius called these beings from the planet *Arshav* the organic formation *intestines*.

"Several days later, when Vesalius was still poking around in the same cadaver, he was mortified to discover that he had originally overlooked *another* native of the planet *Arshav*; their equivalent of a law enforcement agent of the planet Earth.

"These law enforcement agents try to stop this harmful racing of food particles by alerting the humans that it is proceeding within. This is done by the use of certain contractions of the body of the law enforcement agent, sending the particles of food back to the mouth, in order to show the humans what has become of the now useless food substance as a result of the actions of the tube-creatures.

"Vesalius found these law enforcement agents and, as he could not imagine how they might have gotten inside the body unless they also were permanent residents, he decided that they were normally part of the organism, naming this part the *stomach*.

"When he discovered the children of the asteroid-throwing *Lughorts* of the constellation *Parparos* — who practice their adult profession by rolling emissions around inside the bags of these unfortunate humans — and since the effects of the said emissions on human manifestations resemble slightly what are called *emotions*, Vesalius decided to call them *glands*.

"The Sponge-Creatures of the planet *Prana* were called by Vesalius *lungs*.

"Vesalius invented a purpose for anything he found in there. And if he found anything for which he could not invent a use, I don't know of it.

"Another singular invention of his, Gabriel, rests upon the fact that whenever any of these humans goes about some business or other, they do it with a peculiar jerking motion, combined with a sense that whatever they are doing is somehow extremely importance-possessing.

"It seems, from an external point of view, as if they have suddenly been revealed as a sort of 'marionette' whose strings have all of a sudden been pulled.

"This is not at all strange, for within the common presence of each human, can be found one of those creatures from the planet *Ba'aladoux*, called *mamaroux*, who are without doubt the most famous puppeteers of the entire galaxy. Rather than show their new acts by breaking them in at their large cities — thus risking the viewing of their early efforts by critics-at-large, they perform them on Earth.

"In order to try out some new technique, they must of course have a puppet, but cannot transport any item with them when transferring from world to world. Thus they must utilize whatever they can find here that most resembles a puppet, which as you have by now guessed is just that peculiar breed of three-brained beings called *men*.

"Humans of the planet Earth will gladly allow the puppeteers of the planet *Ba'aladoux* to manipulate and direct their actions, simply because they are themselves unable to formulate any real aim. So, naturally, they do not only not resent this interference, but actually welcome it.

"The manipulations and dramas enacted by these *mamaroux* of the planet *Ba'aladoux* are solely responsible for the impulses in humans called by them *dance, sports, cocktail parties, weddings, funeral processions, philosophical lectures, soprano recitals* — in short, anything which requires that they dress in clothing appropriate to the occasion.

"These zany puppeteers were classified and named by Vesalius *the spine*. The equally zany and dramatic actions caused by the puppeteers are called by them *cuteness, nobility,* and *fashionable*, among other names.

"Not only do humans follow, exactly and to the letter all orders issued to them by the puppeteer currently residing within them, but they also copy exactly and by rote, the actions of others following the directions of *their* puppeteers.

"There was yet another instance of parasitic invasion...It is a pity that Vesalius did not give up his belief that these were native to the body, for had he discerned the real nature of this parasite, he could have avoided the catastrophic increase in violence on the planet.

"I refer, of course, to a creature considered the most dangerous in the universe. There is no doubt that Vesalius discovered and catalogued — incorrectly, as usual — this horrifying creature.

"Due to the extreme ecological imbalance in favor of plant life on the planet *Hysteria*, especially the plant life-form called *roses* — of which the dominant species is so fond they risk destruction of their planet in order to grow them, their planet has an unpleasantly heavy atmosphere. In order to thin out this excess of rosy sweet and cloying atmosphere, they dump it into the atmosphere of the planet Earth, transporting it through subspace and then releasing it through the process called by humans 'the action of farting'. Humans do not realize that this gas is not native to the planet Earth.

"More importantly, they have a wild animal on their planet which, had it been allowed to breed unchecked would have destroyed their planet long ago, which said wild animal bears an uncanny resemblance — if only superficially — to humans.

"These wild animals of the planet *Hysteria* manifest only one impulse — to destroy everything in sight not belonging to their own group.

"Ordinarily they would not have the opportunity to cause much destruction on their native planet, because they are never given weapons of any kind — but on the planet Earth, they are the first to be given weapons, and moreover very powerful ones.

"These wild animals are cunningly transported to Earth, and deposited in the bodies of female humans, where they exist during the period of gestation required. They look so similar to human children that they cannot be distinguished from real human children — until they are in possession of a weapon.

"By that time it is too late to send them back to their native planet.

"And so, not only have the *Hysterians* fouled up the Earth's atmosphere with smog resulting from the rosy farts transported to Earth through the bags of humans existing on Earth, but they have also populated the planet with millions — and perhaps even billions — of wild animals, who have since the earliest time of their arrival increased the suffering which must be endured by humans on the planet Earth...

"Of course, Vesalius was not able to mislead *all* succeeding physicians. Some understood real medicine in spite of him.

"One of the later physicians who almost rediscovered the exorcising method of throwing parasites back to their worlds of origin was *Theophrastus Bombastus Von Hohenheim*, who was called by a Latin name, which was later remembered and recorded in history accounts of his life as *Paracelsus* — meaning, perhaps, that he worked alongside someone named 'Celsus'.

"His methods were so remarkable that the other physicians, becoming concerned that they might be compelled to return to medical school, drove him away and tried in every way possible to force him to quit medical practice. Today, of course, physicians have legal protection against unwanted interference from real healers...

"There were still others who almost rediscovered real medicine. A physician named *Mesmer*, and another named *Cagliostro*, and yet another called *Rasputin* came very close — but due to the rampant fear, hostility and superstition of other humans living around them, they were never able to fully develop the practice of real medicine to the point reached by Atlantean physicians.

"But somehow just the tiniest trace of real medicine has survived in the unconscious part of human memory, because today there is performed a ritual similar to the *canopic jar operation*, even if degenerated almost beyond recognition.

"It involves the cutting open of the bag and removal of all interior parasites, but rather than placing them in canopic jars, they give the parasites to playful medical students who like to surprise their fellow students in the dark. And then, with a great deal of ceremony, they bury the now quite empty bag in the dust and forget about it. This modern version of *the canopic jar operation* is called an *autopsy*.

"But, Lord," I asked. "Why don't you send some being of Objective Medicine to go among them and heal them, showing them how to rid themselves of these internal parasites?"

"You did not pay attention, Gabriel, when I explained that they reward all such efforts in the same way that they reward those who attempt to bring an end to all their suffering.

"But even if that were not the case, Gabriel, it would do no good. There have been attempts in the past, many of them. They have always ended in failure, if not disaster, because these humans actually *do not wish to rid themselves of their internal parasites*.

"They do not wish to rid themselves of these parasites because they are proud that the parasitic invasion has taken place within them, and not within other animal forms. This reinforces their belief that the human form is the *best of all possible bags*.

"Another of these parasites that went unrecognized, even to this day, is the being from the planet *Macarios*, which Vesalius called *the skeleton*. These beings are very gregarious, and intensely desire to attend all possible social events.

"Since they are so frightening in appearance to humans, they are forced to disguise themselves by assuming any human body that happens to be currently devoid of a *skeleton* and then, surrounded by the proper 'dressing gown', they are able to attend parties and social gatherings of every sort.

"It is impossible for one of the beings of the planet *Macarios* to attend their social events without the proper uniform, with the exception of one evening, during which, thanks to an old tradition, they may, as is said, 'come as they are', on the holiday *Hallowe'en*.

"I should mention also that in the throats of humans, just below the air and food intake aperture called the mouth, there is a device which Vesalius called *the Adam's Apple*.

This is perhaps the only time when he was at least appropriate in his choice of names. It was properly recorded earlier as *The Apple of Adam*.

"The inhabitants of the planet *Trabalos*, although they have not taken up direct residence as parasites, are responsible for this infernal machine which takes advantage of the human foible of talking incessantly.

"They have connected a small, thin cable through the door between dimensions to a movement-transmitting lever placed inside the *Apple of Adam*, which bobs up and down whenever humans communicate through speech.

"They have hooked up these tiny levers to such devices as *hurdy-gurdies, ferris wheels,* and *washing machines.*

"Ah, me...There is one parasite that they can even see quite clearly, and yet due to their vanity they do nothing to eliminate it.

"This parasitic worm-like being which comes from the planet *Malamat* implants itself under the skin-bag just under the topmost part. Then if lays eggs underneath the skin. When they hatch, they begin to ooze out of the top of the bag.

"They even hire other humans to rearrange these slowly oozing worm-like strands into fashionable arrangements, called by them *coiffure.*

"They hold this *hair* of theirs — if you can believe it — as one of their most prized possessions. Some humans go completely to pieces when even a small portion of it must be cut away for one reason or another. But enough...I will continue my story.

CHAPTER EIGHTEEN

The Attack Of
The Villagers

"The peasants came running out of the woods in order to bring to a permanent stop this unknown enterprise of Harold's which they did not understand — nor did they wish to understand.

"Humans will always and without fail interfere in the lives of others just on the basis that something exists outside their own mental and emotional framework — which they consider threat sufficient.

"Strangely, however, not one of the peasants coming to attack and destroy the fake giant had thought about taking a souvenir or two during the mayhem, perhaps because of the inner feelings induced in their psyches as a result of encountering something strange to them, but also, as a result of its size, producing the sensation of 'awe'. And this is very unusual, Gabriel, because whenever they destroy something of beauty or invention, they usually rip some little part off as a souvenir, which they can sell later in order to keep themselves going until the next opportunity to destroy something comes along.

"Such destructive individuals as these villagers are called by humans, *pressure groups* and are greatly respected and powerful members of the capital of the country America, after which city their first President was named.

"Harold clambered down the ladders from the head, through the midriff, and down the leg, to see if something could be done to save the fake giant from destruction. Just as he reached the ground he saw Friar Feel flying out from the abdomen of the fake giant, moments after the first shock of the attack. The villagers had roped the giant and were trying to pull it down.

"The monk was so relaxed and so round that he did not come to a complete stop until he bounced against the tree at the edge of the clearing. That tree — one of four remaining trees — was now all that was left of what they had called *the forest*, because they had used most of the wood to build the fake giant.

"Harold was relieved when the holy man looked up at him with pleading eyes. The pupils became big and soft, and the monk said softly, as if he lay dying, "Force brandy between my lips!"

"He turned away from the monk, and began working his way back toward the giant. He had been prepared for an emergency such as this, but hadn't realized it until just now.

"When they had rebuilt the giant, they had installed a loudspeaker system to take the place of a center of speech.

"And in the course of building the voice characteristics of the fake giant, they accidentally discovered a secret known only to a few ancient persons of wisdom...

"So they discovered the ancient secret regarding human behavior, which is the law known as 'Bliktiashpo', which can be expressed as: *The Arousal Of Fear In Man As A Result Of Exposure To Unexplained Laughter*.

"When Harold and Irving laughed through the loudspeaker system installed in the fake giant's head, the villagers ran away. After the attack was over, the giant was made ready, and Harold and his companions wheeled it into giant country to make another attempt. But in spite of their improvements and clever vocal apparatus, the fake giant was once again bashed in because the seams were visible on the face.

"Harold expressed concern that the giants would realize what they were doing, because the tale was bound to travel that a fake giant was in the area.

"Relax, Harold," said Irving. "It takes about six or seven months to build a giant, correct?"

"Yes."

"No problem, Harold. Giants don't have an attention span beyond three weeks."

"Gosh," said LeDesirous, "That's two and a half weeks better than I ever did."

"Slowly they drove the smashed gargantuan into the clearing and began to clean up some of the shoddy workmanship that they had hoped to get away with. If the constructed giant were not to be recognized as fake they would have to put in more effort — that was all there was to it.

"Could we please talk one at a time?" asked Harold in the planning meeting. They tried to decide what most needed improvement.

"We could have used more sandwiches." said Moving Hood. "I got to go to the market just before we move this thing out of here, so everything can be fresh."

"I think the hair color is off," said Ham, "And it's parted on the wrong side, and the gears aren't painted."

"Gears? Nobody's going to see the gears!" Harold shouted. "What about the important things?"

"The gears are important," said Moving Hood.

"And *I* see them *all the time*," said Ham.

"When are we going to see some giant women?" asked LeDesirous.

"I have a splitting migraine," said Harold, who went upstairs to the giant's head to rest for a few hours.

"They argued until the next morning, but no one could agree about details. This went on for the next several months, each evening, into early morning — which is why the giant was still only partially finished when they decided to try again.

"When they confronted a giant, probably as a result of tiredness and exhaustion they were not particularly careful with the controls, and the fake giant began to rock back and forth from the waist.

"Orthodox?" asked the real giant.

"But they had all fallen into the fake giant's eyeballs and the motion made it impossible to regain the controls. And so this attempt also — as evidenced by the results on the fake giant's body of expert rearrangement — was a failure, because the real giant walked off when they did not respond.

"We must do something," said Harold. "We are obviously not able to manufacture a convincing giant."

"Sure," said Irving. "But what if we made a giant that didn't *have* to be convincing?"

"What are you getting at?" Harold asked him.

"A fake female giant," explained Irving. "If we build a female giant we don't have to take any care in its construction."

"That's right," said LeDesirous. "As we have all observed, when one is interested in the favors of a lady, who looks at her faults?"

"You really think we can get away with it?" asked Harold.

"Of course," said LeDesirous. "There is hardly a male alive anywhere who will turn down ass."

"I don't think I would have put it quite that way," agreed Irving, "But that *is* the essence of the situation."

"So they reconstructed the fake giant along female lines. That is, they added the most vital part of feminine anatomy, the breasts. When the villagers returned to try to destroy the fake giant once again, they retreated without need for the laughing machine.

"Excuse me, madam," the headman of the village said, as he turned to run back to town.

"We have succeeded!" announced Harold.

"It fooled the *villagers*, all right," said Friar Feel. "But is it good enough to convince a *giant*?"

"When they brought the fake female giant up to a real giant, the giant became so hopeful of sexual conquest that he did not notice the places where the seams met in the center of the face. In short, his full attention was focused in the area of the chest.

"Say, big boy," chirped Harold in his best falsetto voice, "What's the secret of gianthood?"

"Haw Haw," the giant guffawed, removing its head. Standing on the platform opposite them, Harold and his companions could see plainly that it had been a fake also, peopled by ordinary humans. They had been so awe-struck by the giants that they had never noticed that *all* giants have seams showing where they are sewn together. In short, there were no giants in the land of giants, just ordinary folks inside giant bodies.

"We're *all* fakes!" Harold declared.

"Just at that moment everything went hazy again." The Lord sat back, and drew out another cigarette.

CHAPTER NINETEEN

The Aftermath

"That's *it*?" I asked incredulously. "That's the end of the story?"

"Yep — that's it," he grinned.

"I realize, Lord," I said, "that once again I have been had."

"Maybe now you'd like to eat?" He inquired. He gazed off into the distance — seeming to pierce the very endlessness of space. One would think that all the universe had been contained within that tent in which we sat together conversing.

"No, Lord, not just yet. I do not understand what happened to Harold of Cummingood."

"What don't you understand about it, Gabriel?" he asked.

"Well, to tell you the truth, I must have blacked out on the end of the story."

"Maybe I can explain it by telling you about something that happened to me on one of my early visits to the planet Earth."

"Perhaps, Lord. And since I am already well aware that there is the possibility now at this very moment as a result of such explanations from you regarding your work here toward

the essential natures of these humans residing on the planet
Earth for new understanding and assimilation of formerly
acquired data which may not have formed as yet within
myself, I will now actively create within myself the necessary
arousal of all centers in order to fully receive all such data at
their exact points of origin.''

"That's good, Gabriel, and while you are at it, you should
pay attention. Ready?'' The Lord asked, after I had prepared
myself in this way.

"Yes, Lord...Shoot.''

The Lord drew a .32 calibre 'Saturday night special' from
the locker under His bunk and aimed it at my forehead.

"Not like *that*, Lord!'' I said. "I meant that it was okay to
go ahead and tell the story.''

"Oh,'' He said. He put the pistol back inside the locker
and I breathed a deep sigh of relief.

"Was that a sigh of relief I just heard?'' The Lord asked in
a cunning tone.

"Yes, Lord,'' I admitted. "I was slightly concerned for the
continued existence of this planetary body. I did not want to
miss the story, and without it I would have been compelled to
return to wardrobe for another.''

"You're not becoming attached to that one, are you?'' He
asked in a suspicious tone.

"No, Lord, really, I'm not. I just wanted to hear the
story.''

"Okay, Gabe, I'll let you off this time...But if you show any
sign of attachment...''

"I know, Lord. Back to the drawing board.''

"You could have borrowed another one from me in the
event of an accident. I always carry several spares with me
whenever I visit the planet Earth, having learned from
previous encounters here how careless humans are with the
bodies of my messengers — most of which have been
destroyed with not the slightest qualm or respect for the cost
and effort on my part to send them again.''

CHAPTER TWENTY

First Descent On Gnaripogipog

"When I first decided to visit the country of *Gnaripogipog*, it seemed like a good idea at the time to appear in accordance with the customary beliefs of the inhabitants regarding my attributes. Therefore I wore the *Blue Surge Suit*, which they call *Saint Krishna*."

"I thought I noticed it missing in the wardrobe department, Lord," I said.

"Yes, thanks to the reactions of these humans existing on the planet Earth, that exact costume is no longer available for use. Due to certain aggressive tendencies and jealous habits of theirs, I lost it in the scuffle, and all because of a little misunderstanding regarding the sexual behavior of a few thousand cowgirls," He said, His voice unusually soft and thoughtful.

"I had already constated to myself that unless I could deliver some form of conscious shock to the *Gnaripogipogians* they would in a few years cease entirely to develop in Essence and would become completely *psyche beings* — using only their minds and imaginary emotions. As it was, they only moved their mental, emotional and physical muscles in rigid postures and patterns long ago established by their society, and as a result were unable to activate Essence after having reached the age of only five years.

"I knew that if things continued in this way without change of some kind, they would inevitably sink into a state of 'American Apathy', from which, as you know, there is no hope of escape by ordinary means.

"I had for many years observed that they had already become quite dead in the centers of thinking, feeling, and moving...but that they were still somehow at least a little alive in the center of reproduction. I resolved to deliver the conscious shock to that center, hoping that it would arouse the other centers back to life.

"My first problem in this regard was to somehow engage in sex with several thousand of their females and deliver to them through this action the aforementioned conscious shock, which they could then pass on to their males, who in turn could pass it on to other females, as is their custom — although they will not admit it.

"And so I found for this purpose several thousand milkmaids, or 'cow-girls', who had as their being-task the chore of milking cows — ten thousand of them, to be exact, all of whom I had sex with in exactly the manner most pleasing to each."

"Lord..." I said in a shocked tone. "You had sex with ten thousand cows?"

"No. Gabriel, I had sex with ten thousand *milkmaids* — simultaneously..." He added, with His eyes half-lidded, staring dreamily off into space.

"Good Lord!" I said, "So to speak. That must have been quite a problem to get all those young ladies to agree to have sex with you."

"What? No — you don't understand humans, Gabriel. That wasn't the problem. They all agreed in a moment. Agreement for the enactment of a pleasure sensation is *never* a problem among humans.

"I had in a previous descent upon the planet Earth noted

that during their sexual contact with each other there was aroused in them those real feelings associated ordinarily with the experience of the Real World and that this impulse could be aroused by even the suggestion of the possibility of future sex.

"This impulse could form in them — even if only on a temporary basis — the potential for conscious life.

"In accordance with this plan of mine I was constrained to bring into the ordinary habitual function of sex the added factor of *intentional suffering* — the deliberate decision to not release the substances 'Eksohari' and 'Protohari' unconsciously, which are under ordinary conditions of sexual contact released automatically.

"This action on their part of not releasing these substances unconsciously resulted in the said sexual contact altering itself into a series of states in which the individuals taking part 'rose above themselves' — that is to say, above their ordinary animal natures — into a realm in which they were able to sense the whole process of life and death, and all subsequent experiences following the transition of their essential beings into the non-vibratory cosmos called 'The Void'.

"In order to fully help them for their own permanent development through this factor resulting in them from receiving the impressions of the 'Sacred Recognition of Reality', they would not only have to become aware of the process of all life in all natural formations existing around them, but also of the inevitable cessation of all forms of life — including their own — existing around them at the same time.

"And so I introduced the system of performing their reproductive actions *in harmony with the beginning and end of life*. That is, within each member of the coincidental performance similar to that used for reproduction of the species there was stimulated through certain exercises and visualizations a full memory, perception, and sensation of the conception, fetal and embryonic growth, emergence into the so-called 'outer world' of the child, and the cessation, burial, and subsequent transformation of the planetary body, along with the perception, sensation and knowledge inherent in the evolution or dissipation of the Essence, depending upon its development, if any. As a result, each time they had sex it was like being born, living and dying all at once.

"But they entirely misunderstood my instructions.

"They came also to believe, in accordance with this misunderstanding psyche of theirs, that during the process of reproduction they ought by all means to try to cause in themselves the deliberate overpowering of all automatic functions of instinct. That is to say, they tried to kill themselves through 'spinal meditation' during the process of sex.

"And in order to add even more madness to this already madcap mish-mosh, they decided, according to another idea of theirs that 'it doesn't hurt to throw in a little something for the postman and if there's enough for the butcher, put that in, too'...They decided that when they died they ought to put in a little 'extra energy' so that they could be *certain* to achieve transformation...In accordance with this idea, they decided to throw in the living or freshly deceased planetary bodies of the immediate family along with the planetary body of the male head of the household — particularly the wife — with the exception of possible heirs and alternate nephews in line for succession.

"And the only reason heirs and nephews were excused from this was the short life expectancy due to the disaster to their psyches which had occurred a few years earlier when I had to replace their moon — which had broken away from the main body of their planet — with a hastily constructed substitute, which said replacement I was constrained through lack of time to push into place using a large middle finger made especially by the prop department just for the occasion. Had I not done so, the planet would have burst asunder.

"Not only did they form in themselves the unfortunate habit of placing the planetary bodies of wives, servants, and household slaves, who up until the date of death of the boss were in quite good health, into the tombs of their dead aristocracy, but they also decided to throw in the household pets, bushels of grain and fruit, and furniture — not to mention the best china in the house!

"But the unwilling and sudden cessation of the active formation of the planetary bodies of the servants, slaves, family, and household pets who did not voluntarily discontinue their ordinary existence in the world cannot possibly help the deceased in accomplishing transformation — no additional obligation is discharged as a result of uniting the deaths of these extra bodies to that of the power-possessing deceased person.

"After the advent of the dynasty of the family of rulers named *Purnadun*, this custom of stuffing the tomb with friends, slaves, and relatives buried before their normal time of retirement from the world with the deceased, due to this misunderstanding regarding my instructions to them, was changed by the intervention of the first independently powerful queen of that country, who recognized her own certain danger if her husband should fall victim to the inevitable cessation of bodily functions of the planetary form before she herself had satisfactorily completed her 'tour of duty' here on Earth.

"And rather than place within the tomb the actual bodies of relatives, servants, slaves, pets, and fruits, vegetables and furniture, she caused to be placed instead in the said tombs carved wooden and alabaster sandstone substitutes. At first because it was considerably more expensive then simply dumping in the bodies of relatives and slaves, only the rich could afford to make such substitutions.

"But since the poor believed in this afterlife and wished to insure their continued existence also — and increase their prosperity — in the afterworld, they developed a very urgent motivation to find some way to procure similar afterlife servants for themselves.

"Real estate values in the Necropolis were already enough of a burden. So it was that they devised little clay 'cookie figures' covered with a glaze called *faience*, which could be mass-produced and therefore could be used in a great quantity for very little money. At first even these little mass-produced cookie figures for the middle class families were quite elegant, and had a beauty all their own.

"When the practice became popular, many unskilled artisans appeared, with the very first 'Schachermacher-Shops' and the quality rapidly degenerated. Factories for the creation of *Baked-Mud Servants, Clay Slaves* and *Cookie-Wives* sprang up everywhere. Soon these little figures were stamped out in wholesale fashion, by the tens of thousands.

"Vendors of these almost-amorphous blobs began to appear everywhere in the vicinity of their burial grounds, hawking these new mass-produced items which can only be described as somehow resembling something found only in a swamp.

"I have often wondered what the expressions of these deceased persons would be if I could arrange for them to awaken in this imaginary world to come of theirs, finding themselves surrounded by thousands of these lumpy little miscreations of theirs.

"I came to realize that before I could re-introduce the correct instructions given by me to them previously, I could not stop completely, but only alter, those habits already acquired by them, according to another little abnormality of theirs which causes them to manifest anything habitual whether appropriate or not, and resist its replacement with another habit, and to simply obey compulsively all habits already within them through sheer momentum.

"Only after an old habit is replaced with another habit can a genuinely new pattern be introduced into their common existences for any purpose whatever. I had constated to myself that in order to bring this about, the restorial action of a deliberately introduced special shock would be required — of sufficient force that it would bring everything within them to a dead halt.

"At first, rather than arouse indirectly in the Gnaripogi-pogians the Sacred impulse *To Be Continually Aware Of All Life Proceeding Everywhere At Once*, through the usual methods as had been my custom, I had the idea to use a long-established habit already present within them. In this way I would not have to persuade them to give up one habit and adopt an entirely new one — a task proven to be impossible under any conditions whatever.

"In order to understand what I did and why I did it, it is necessary to be aware that among humans, nothing reminds them more of the process of life and death than their means of reproducing themselves, and there is nothing more powerful in this regard than the sudden confrontation with a male reproductive organ...and the larger the organ, the more strongly they receive the said sensation, arousing within them the aforementioned sacred impulse *To Be Continually Aware Of All Life Proceeding Everywhere At Once*.

"The addition of a face on the tip of the penis adds only a little to the already existing suggestion of a face at the tip of these organic formations of theirs, at the sight of which there is aroused in them immediately *the sensation of mystery-and-impending-doom*.

"And so in accordance with the said abnormality of theirs regarding the sensation aroused at the sight of a penis, I caused to be carved to my exact specifications thousands of enormous stone columns resembling precisely a huge male reproductive organ, but with *four* faces on the tip, rather than just one, on the basis of another abnormality in the psyches which they express in the following way: 'If *one* inch of chrome is good, then *ten* inches of chrome is *ten* times as good.'

"In order to provide a constant reminder and thus to assist the assimilation of this impulse, I arranged the opening of certain *clubs of a different kind*, in which the process of regeneration of the species could be performed in accordance with the precise instructions given by me directly to the aforementioned milkmaids.

"Corresponding with the formation of these *clubs of a different kind*, I caused the erection — you should pardon the expression — of stone columns, called *Lats*, all over the countryside of Gnaripogipog.

"And at the top of each of these stone columns there was originally a carving of a lion, a bull, an eagle, and the head of a virgin. At first the sight of these solid stone columns caused in everyone the immediate sensations of 'mystery' and 'awe', provoking the inner sensing of life as a complete cycle of existence.

"This was continually reinforced through membership in the said *clubs of a different kind* set up by me. Everything seemed to be going very well, and I thought that by the following year this problem would be completely solved. But I had not counted on still another peculiar function in the abnormally constructed human psyche...Through use and exposure, sex became for them uninteresting and boring, and they became completely disinterested in the reproduction of their species. Membership in the clubs dropped almost to zero...Almost to zero, but not quite.

"The only members remaining in the clubs were those who had been forced through early cultural training to develop a completely fixated psyche concentrated entirely on what is called *the Fox-Trot*, while still very young. I was unwilling under the new circumstances to continue the meetings necessary for the reinforcement of the message contained in the stone columns, and so I left the country Gnaripogipog.

"Soon after that, everyone and his brother had completely forgotten what the stone columns were intended to accomplish — that is, they forgot, until one day a farmer by the name of Mr. Shiva, out with his oxen plowing the field, was stopped by one of these stone columns.

"Now, how in heck am I going to get this thing out of the way?" he mused. "I obviously can't move it, and it ain't no good for nothin' anyway..." and as his sullen thoughts flowed, he suddenly had an inspiration...

"This inspiration of his was to invent an entirely new religion based upon these stone columns. He decided to form a priesthood which had exclusive interview rights with the gods of the Lats. Along with this, he also invented a set of beliefs for the basic philosophy of this religion of his — the more esoteric of which could be understood only by Mr. Shiva himself.

"He announced the discovery of paper-thin gold tablets — buried in the mud — which told the real meaning of the stone columns. He explained that the four heads atop the Lats were not placed there to arouse in humans the impulses of *fortitude, courage, vision* and *purity*, as I had originally intended, but were actually intended to divide the planet into four separate sections, each with its own tribe of humans on it, intended by 'Mr. God' to maintain racial purity.

"He told his followers that the Earth had been intended to be divided into four main parts each with its own special race of humans. And he called each of these four parts of the Earth *One Quarter.*

"Along with this, he invented a mantra for his followers to use as they drove out those not belonging to the correct denomination for that particular quarter of the planet, which when translated into our own tongue comes out as: *Would You Buy It For A Quarter?*

"He gave this mantra to those beings of *Type One* who joined his new religion after having paid the usual fee for membership, of course.

"He also gave a second mantra to *Type Two* initiates — those who were so fiercely loyal that they would do anything for the establishment of this new religion of his. This second mantra was based on the fact that the stone columns vaguely resembled sticks shoved into the ground. This second mantra given to *Type Two* initiates can be translated in our language as: *Take it and stick it!*

"He caused to be manufactured for his congregation special smaller versions of the stone columns, carved out of *Ironwood*, with just one small alteration from the original...in place of the head of a virgin, he had carved into these smaller wooden Lats his own — idealized, of course — likeness.

"And whenever someone would ask about the special clubs started by me earlier in relation to these stone columns, he would bend toward them in a fatherly way, and handing the inquirer one of these little wooden carvings resembling a stone Lat, he would say in his most soothing tone:

"Never mind, child...Here is a *new* club, more suitable for our own times and people...Here is *a club of a different kind.*"

"Eventually, because his followers could not think of any other use for these little wooden clubs given to them by Mr. Shiva, they began to use them to rearrange the forms of those beings who would neither agree with, nor become members of, this new religion of theirs, into which they had been, as they believed, *born again.*

"Soon they became so enthused about this method of converting others to their religion that they began to use the mantras given to them by Mr. Shiva as battle cries.

"Due to this aggressive behavior in the said application of miniature ironwood Lats, rather than associate their process of reproduction with the sensing of all life proceeding everywhere all at once, they instead automatically associated it with the deliberate murder of members of their own species who did not agree with their unique beliefs, performing these aggressive acts upon each other with the degree of enthusiasm and glee only understandable to other humans, in accordance with their chief aphorism, or wise saying: *Better it should happen to you than it should happen to me...*

"Naturally, his followers would not allow Mr. Shiva to keep them permanently ignorant of the inner mysteries of his invented religion, and since he had since its founding constated a new aim — that is, to have his new religion continue past the death of his planetary body, assuring him immortality in at least *some* form, if not in reality, this conformed to his own aim.

"At first he had only wished for some way to gain the income necessary for the attainment of certain items for which he had formed during childhood an urgent desire; but afterward he began to wish for a little something more. But, since he had no way to perfect his Essence-body, he knew — although only unconsciously — that he had to depend upon another, quite ordinary, kind of immortality.

"And so, owing to this new impulse of his, he resolved to pass on to his closest associates all the high inner mysteries of his new religion. Unfortunately, he had not yet formulated a single inner mystery, even to himself...

"Having constated this requirement for himself for the perpetuation of his memory and influence over future generations, he retired to his lounge in order to compose for them a few inner mysteries. In regard to the specific composition, he had more or less the same problem as had Scheherezade. He was constrained to invent on the spot a few believable cosmic principles which would seem so wonderfully real that the advanced initiates waiting in the next room would 'buy it for a quarter'...but...

"Just at the moment when Mr. Shiva was about to impart those secrets made up by him, known *only* by him and by no one else, having just a few moments before this ingested a large amount of *roast pork guy ding*, without the proper Essence-enjoyment...that is to say, unconsciously...and also due to the combined results of haste, psychophysical turmoil, and stress caused by his unfortunately unbreakable habit of fearing for his life, a piece of pork became lodged in his throat, and he choked to death before he could utter a single inner mystery.

"As a result of this, the separation of his astral body from the planetary body was even worse than usual.

"He had not had time to transmit even one little inner mystery to his followers, but this little disappointment had no effect whatever on the continuation of the *Shiva Movement*. He had not known that his followers would continue completely automatically just through the force of momentum. This new, quite profitable, religion of his had already for some reason become an unbreakable habit with its followers.

"In fact, the force of the movement actually increased after his untimely demise, due to another abnormality in the psyches of humans on Earth, which can be said in our language as: *If I don't know what it is, and can never know what it is, it must be something grand.*

"And so the *Shiva Movement* carries on into the present day, thus interfering permanently in any efforts on my part in behalf of the inhabitants of the country of Gnaripogipog, who, as it turned out, would have been much better off without my intervention, since this new religion is even more destructive to the development of their Essences than simple *American Apathy*. But fortunately I had another new idea...This time a really Crackerjack Plan!''

CHAPTER TWENTY-ONE

The Country Of Nakhnik

"I had at least one more possible tactic remaining to me regarding the forced Essence-development of those darn *Gnaripogipogians*, thanks to two habits deeply ingrained in them which could be adapted to my purposes.

"First, they had an unreasoning respect for the inhabitants of the land just to the north of their country, holding them in great reverence and admiration, even though they knew nothing about them other than travelers' rumors, since they lived far apart and had little direct contact.

"About these almost mythical inhabitants of the northern country, the land called *Nakhnik*, they would believe anything — most of all anything impossible for ordinary humans — and thus could be counted on to imitate anything coming from the country *Nakhnik*.

"Secondly, they had formed in themselves the uncontrollable habit to amuse themselves by beating time on pots, pans, drums and cymbals, strumming strings, blowing horns, reeds and whistles, and, in short, making all kinds of noises stimulating corresponding vibrations pleasing to themselves within their planetary bodies.

"I knew that these two impulses of theirs would continue and form naturally a foundation for the plan I had in mind to correct the previous failure.

"In order for my plan to succeed, the Gnaripogipogians would have to accept the influence of the northern people of *Nakhnik* in a particular manner calculated by me, according to yet another abnormal factor in the psyches of humans of the planet Earth — the singular inability to distinguish between something that occurred in the past, and something which is occurring in the present.

"In accordance with this peculiarity of the human psyche, I knew that the planetary body could be depended upon to adjust itself automatically to any reality suggested by vibrations contained in music *as if that reality actually were proceeding in the present*. Through experiments, I determined that the human organism can be persuaded to alter its form, and the mind its contents, through the influence of certain sound vibrations and percussive shocks.

"For instance, by making a particular *chord*, a combination of single notes and harmonics of prime notes, one can raise a welt on the skin or conversely eliminate a cancerous growth. With another combination of notes one can alter the bone formation by convincing the body that it is a formation of being existing on an entirely different planet.

"I should also be able to depend upon the mechanical continuation of whatever musical notation I introduced, as long as I included with it some form of entertainment. Accordingly, I intermingled these sounds with a form of dancing called by them 'sacred'.

"For the notation of the dances, I used a special alphabet invented by me for the purpose of making shorthand symbols for each movement and each posture of the arm, hand, leg, trunk, and facial expression.

"This system had a double use. I could choreograph dance movements, and at the same time encode a system of aphorisms, which could be retranslated by acting out each of the letter combinations. Within the said dance movements I could insert, letter for letter, the basic knowledge of Essence development.

"I did this knowing that governments and churches periodically spring up which forbid the transmission of knowledge.

"Thus by concealing knowledge in the form of dance, I could assure myself that they would continue into the future unnoticed, and yet could be read by anyone who knew the alphabet notation of the planetary body in its various positions.

"By introducing certain chords and movements into the music and dance coming out of the northern country of *Nakhnik* to the southern country of *Gnaripogipog*, the southerners would then automatically imitate the music and dance of their respected, revered, and admired neighbors — and moreover, would copy them verbatim, not daring to alter anything emanating from such miraculous beings.

"This special music would, when played in the exact sequence outlined by me according to Objective Law, cause an automatic compensating adjustment in planetary bodies and minds corresponding to the reality suggested by the vibrations contained in the objective music.

"Just as I had hoped, the people of the country of *Gnaripogipog* immediately adopted this new form of musical expression.

"I knew that if this plan of mine succeeded, I could later introduce sounds suggesting all areas of Real Life.

"Soon everyone in the country of *Gnaripogipog* was able to exist in — and directly experience — the Real World in an active Essence state.

"If this had continued, all humans everywhere would soon have become inhabitants of the Real World, but as you have probably guessed by now, this new factor consciously introduced by me was soon altered by yet another of their seemingly endless stream of abnormal habits — something I had not counted on to bring all this to a halt.

"This other, unforeseen habit of theirs was the uncontrollable urge to 'Make something new, always something new, no matter what!'

"And so, in accordance with this other little abnormality of theirs, about which I had forgotten completely up until then, they altered the sequence of the chords, then the sequence of the dance, and finally the music and the movements altogether so that they were more pleasing to them.

"Even though they altered the form and content, thus eliminating its beneficial effect, they continued to call it by the same name as before, and today it still bears the name *Surparar*, which translates to our own tongue as: *Futile dances to imaginary music.*"

CHAPTER TWENTY-TWO

What Happened To Harold?

"I understand completely what you have been trying to explain to me through the analogy of that story, Lord," I said. "But it still leaves me in the dark about what happened to Harold."

"You ignorant twit!" His voice was silky. "You do not need to know anything about this. It would simply serve to satisfy your already overwrought imagination and curiosity."

"But Lord..." I said.

"Lord me no Lords! And do not interject your vague thoughts — I will tell you about it if only to shut you up! Otherwise I have a feeling I will not hear the end of this for some time to come..."

"Thank you, Lord."

"In the course of human events, it eventually became necessary for me to encapsulate their world into a completely mechanical process. These beings on their typically circuitous paths, were already quite destructive.

"This mechanical format of existence for humans is all that prevents them from destroying the objective pattern of their world, and that of all forms. The problem for them is that although the Essence is immortal, it is usually stupid, while the body and psyche are very intelligent but limited in duration to the life of the planetary body, which, even though it recurs endlessly, is not always occupied by the same being, for as soon as the body has run down through entropic failure the Essence separates from it, leaving it to blend once again with the planetary body from which it arose...

"Unless the being who has up to that time inhabited that planetary body has transformed the Essence into an active and permanent entity in which habits have been formed consciously along certain definite lines...thus helping to create the subtle body required for the placement of a soul, and in that way justifying and completing my hopes for humans on the planet Earth...*Do you understand what I am trying to tell you, Gabriel?*"

"Yes, Lord, but what happened to Harold?"

The Lord compassionately drove his right knee smartly into my groin, which is an already agreed-upon signal between us that I had in some way failed to comprehend exactly what he had been saying.

"This can only mean one thing, Gabriel," He said. "A basic inability to grasp the subject at hand — and far worse, since a simple intellectual understanding of these ideas is of no value, *an example of vivifying force will have to be used.*"

The Lord sat back and waited for that bit of information to sink in, and I, sure that I had already received sufficient data at that moment for the attainment of a new gradation of reason one degree above Ankhlad, periodically felt the top of my head for any sign of the appropriate horns, which I expected imminently, according to some very intricate calculations using the old *Gregorian calendar* and some *litmus paper*.

But all I got for my trouble was scalp flakes on the fingertips — and suddenly I realized that after all this time I still had no idea what had happened to Harold.

"My Dear Lord," I said in as calm a tone as I could muster, "I am terribly sorry, but I have just realized that there has been a certain omission in the conversation which has been proceeding between us...That is to say, you have not yet completed the story of Harold of..."

I realized at that moment with a sudden twinge of horror that The Lord showed every indication of having assumed my degree of reason — three degrees lower than His usual Absolute Reason!

"Lord," I said to Him, "Those are my horns you are wearing, I believe..." and waited for Him to hand them over.

"Just a little joke, Gabriel," He said.

"That was not funny, Lord," I said. "These horns are not to play around with. Besides," I continued, "they're mine." He gave them to me.

"*That* you call a sense of humor?" He asked in a hurt tone.

"Hey, I worked hard for these, Lord," I said, placing them on my head.

Then everyone came into the tent and sang 'For He's A Jolly Good Fellow!' and gave me a gold watch.

When they left, I turned toward Him once more, to hear what He might have to say to me on this auspicious occasion.

But I realized with a sudden shock that He had stopped speaking some time ago, and that His narrative must have come to a point of completion without my awareness.

I understood with a wave of cold sweat that He intended to go no further in His discourse, and that as far as He was concerned, the conversation was over.

I had been squirming to find out what had happened to Harold, and now it seemed that I would never know. But for the first time since the subject had arisen, a profound calm proceeded within me regarding this subject, and gazing at Him with tears of gratitude for His labors on behalf of beings everywhere, I whispered "Thank you, Lord...Thank you for being."

And, with a smile of even for Him unusual beneficence and Essence-love, He gave up His planetary existence.

May God Have Mercy
Upon The Sinner
Who Wrote This Book
of Wiseacrings and Foolishness.

CHAPTER TWENTY-THREE

The Lord's Last Gasp

With a blinking of His dark, bloodshot eyes, and a twitch of His big bulbous nose, The Lord heaved a sigh, and looking up at me asked: "Where am I?"

"On Earth, Lord, in the tent on Sinai Memorial Mountain."

"Hmmm," He said to Himself, "That indicates that my calculations were incorrect, and that my work in this sector is not quite complete."

Having so said, He rose and walked around the tent, and then sat back down on the pillows. I anticipated that He would wish some form of refreshment upon His Miraculous Recovery, and so obtained for Him a large glass and filled it with ice-cold water. He took a small sip, spat it out on the dusty floor of the tent, and said, "Now that you have demonstrated that the glass is indeed clean, by leaving in it the exact water with which it was washed, please be so kind as to bring me something in this now sufficiently sterile container suitable for the proper celebration of my unexpected continuation of life!"

I brought some French apple brandy, which He gulped down without any sign of discomfort.

"Ah, there is no doubt about it," He said. "This liquid refreshment is 'the cat's whiskers' for celebrating the resurrection of this body."

"Oh, Lord," I anxiously exclaimed, "you aren't going to do it again? Not another *Appearance To Humanity*? You certainly don't intend to do anything more than you already have for these petrified, rock-headed, fear-driven, vain, ignorant, savage, brutal..."

I would have gone on, but The Lord quieted me with a wave of His forearm across my chops, which — as already agreed between us — signifies 'Enough'.

"Yes, that is what I am going to do...And furthermore, if I run into something unexpected, I hope that you and the rest of the angelic host will see it through to the end."

"I am honored by your trust, Lord," I said with my teeth chattering for some reason I could not fathom. "But exactly what do you intend to do this time?"

"Oh, it doesn't matter..." He said, "...The fact is that no one will pay much attention anyway."

"But Lord, I do not understand. We both know that the humans on this planet are savage monsters. And what do you mean when you say that anything you do will be ignored...Or is that what you said?" I was so confused that I found it impossible to sort out the conversation that had preceded this exchange.

"One thing at a time, *boychik*," He said, laughing. "I am not so foolish as to intentionally become a victim of these Earth creatures' desire to bring all my Heavenly Messengers to martyrdom."

"Can you give me a hint about what you're going to do?" I asked.

"I will do more than that, Gabriel. As you may be one of the necessary individuals required by me for the enactment of the said announcement, I should by all means now explain my plan to you in detail.

"As you are already aware, Gabriel, the humans on this

planet now occupy themselves with commerce to the degree that most of them have become paper-shufflers to such an extent that they no longer have a direct relationship with the livingness of their planet.

"And so when they arrive home after such meaningless labors, they have not used up their daily quantity of energy allotted for the purpose of livelihood. As a result, they become agitated and uncomfortable, and wish to raise 'some kind of heck' before retiring for the night, arousing themselves to a fever pitch at any rate sufficiently to allow them to walk over to the radio and turn it on, and then sit back and read the newspaper for hours, until finally sleep overtakes them in the middle of the sports section.

"In this way they seek some release from an over-abundance of energy. You should understand, my boy, that to them, entertainment consists largely of placing lampshades atop their empty heads, and throwing whipped cream pies in each other's faces.

"To make certain that I will not become a victim as were all my Messengers in the past, I could take the disguise of such so-called 'talent', so respected among these humans that they would never crucify one of their entertainers for fear of eternal boredom..." He said, lapsing off into a deep reverie which humans existing on Earth would call a *grand mal seizure*, finally passing out cold on the floor...

"No!" He said suddenly, rising halfway toward the pillows nearby, "I will make my announcement directly! Do you know where I can get a red robe, some sandals, and a white ass?"

I mentioned that this particular presentation had been done before.

"Oh, pish-tush," He said. "It's always been one of my best effects...This will take some thought," He said, lapsing once again into a deep state of reverie.

Just as I raised the tent flaps to walk out, he yelled at me to come back inside.

"Not so fast, you impatient young pup!" He snapped. I could see from His countenance that He wasn't quite finished with our discussion, and so I sat down next to Him once again.

"As I was saying, becoming a star is not the solution...What time is it?"

"Four o'clock Thursday," I replied, without thinking.

"No, no, you idiot! Local time!" I told Him.

"Perhaps it might help if I made a few suggestions?" I offered timidly.

"Might, at that," He said. "Go ahead."

"Well, Lord, it would help if I knew what the message was going to be."

"You're just trying to steal my secrets!" He screamed, and ran out of the tent. I boiled some cabbage and threw it out after Him.

"Hello," said The Lord as He re-entered the tent. "So you're the new one?" I realized that He was performing Sacred Teaching and decided to play along with it.

"The message I intend to announce is: *The Quick Brown Fox Jumps Over The Lazy Dog.*"

"What does that mean, Lord?" I asked in some dismay.

"Let him who has ears to hear, let him hear!" And so saying He gave up His material form once again.

"And one more thing..." He said, sitting up supporting Himself on one elbow. "...Keep your nose clean!" And then He once again expired. "And don't take any wooden nickels," He added, sitting up once more. It was but a moment later that He stirred once again, saying, "Birds of a feather flock together!" And then with a final shuddering gasp, He died.

"But have a shovel handy, and don't forget to flush the toilet!" He added, and then at last was gone.

I turned away to leave, blissfully aware that He was now back in His Eternal Resting Place, and so with a final look around, I left the tent, with His last words whispering in the wind.

"And don't slam the tent flaps!" I heard Him whine as I walked away. Suddenly He burst out of the tent and began running after me as I strode off into the cold night air, His barbed tail flapping in the breeze.

"Wait, Gabriel!" He shouted, and I waited for Him to catch up.

"Yes, Lord?" I asked, impatient to be on my way.

"I forgot to tell you what happened to Harold! I cannot rest until that knowledge has been definitely imparted to you!"

"Really?" I asked coldly, continuing once again to walk down the hill.

"Yes, yes," He said, endeavoring to keep pace with my firm stride.

"Well?" I asked, stopping suddenly in front of Him, not particularly eager to receive a useless bit of information which could only confuse the mission given to me by Him.

"You just want to steal my secrets!" He bellowed, running into the desert below.

I stood there for a moment...then I realized that it was true — I *did* want to steal His secrets! I ran after Him as fast as I could...

...And found myself in a museum in the city of *Cairo*. There in ancient glyphs was the message: "Gabriel, if you want to see me, I'll be at the Cafe in the bazaar next to this museum."

He sat with several tradesmen at one of the outdoor tables. "Ah," He said at my approach. "You're just in time to hear this...Gentlemen, if you please..."

Each of His guests mechanically repeated in his own tongue: *The Quick Brown Fox Jumps Over The Lazy Dog.* The Lord nodded enthusiastically, and bid them good day, as they left the table.

"Well, my boy," He said to me at last. "As you can see, I have not been idle since we last saw each other. All over the world my message — even though not yet understood — is being disseminated. Meanwhile, what have you been doing to help?"

"I've been looking for you, Lord," I admitted.

"You would have done better if you had gotten right to work," He admonished. "It was just luck that we met here. In another hour I would have been gone. You might have had to follow my notes for a long time and still not found me. However, had you begun work, we would certainly have met. But enough — we have things to do that cannot wait."

So saying, The Lord began to screech in an obnoxiously high-pitched voice, and waving a large insect between His thumb and forefinger, gestured wildly at the head waiter.

"A cockroach!" He screamed. "A cockroach in my soup!"

But it didn't work, and I had to pay for the meal.

We walked out of the restaurant in front of the glares of the waiters and the cashier. "We can get this message of mine placed into all secretarial and typing schools, and we can take employment as 'typewriter repairmen', leaving scraps of paper in the machines which contain my new message.

"As it is human nature to copy anything they see, they will think that it is an objective test of a typewriter's function."

"Say, Lord," I said. "It has just occurred to me that there's more to all this than you've been telling me."

"Why, whatever do you mean, Gabriel?" He gently inquired.

"I mean all this story-telling, lunch with those business-men, all of it. You've been beating around the bush, so to speak," I accused.

"I was only trying to ease the shock before I told you about it, Gabriel," He said.

"Oh, gracious me..." I said. "What is it?"

"Listen, Gabriel, not every effort can be a crackerjack."

"Oh, no! For heaven's sake, Lord, drop the other shoe! What's gone wrong *this* time?"

"Nothing much," He said, kicking the sand below His feet in an offhand manner.

"Tell me!" I insisted.

"Well, Gabriel..."

"Yes?"

"How soon do you think you could muster the entire Heavenly Host?" He muttered.

"What?" I shouted. "The entire Heavenly Host? That must mean that this is a 'crackerjack emergency'! Maybe just a few angels and archangels...? Things can't have gotten *that* bad!"

"Oh?" He replied. He was in a pretty mellow mood, but that doesn't signify anything, since no matter what happens He survives it all, and so naturally He doesn't identify with it as we lesser beings subject to non-Absolute laws do.

"Why *can't* things have gone that wrong?" He asked mildly.

"Come on, Lord! I can take it!" I said, gritting my teeth. "What happened?"

"It's the end of the entire cosmos," He said pleasantly, with that shy little smile He reserves just for such statements.

"What?" I cried.

"Easy come, easy go," He shrugged philosophically.

"That's easy for *you* to say, Lord."

"Maybe we can still save some part of it, Gabriel," He offered cheerfully.

"Oh, yeah? How?" I wanted to know.

"How soon did you say you could assemble the Heavenly Host?"

"Don't you have any plan at all?"

"Well, I thought I might replace the human population with something a little less violent and destructive," He mused.

"Isn't that a bit drastic?" I asked. "Willikers, Lord, you've really done it this time!"

"Oh, I wouldn't get into an uproar about it, Gabriel."

"My Aunt Mary, I won't get into an uproar about it! You think *this* is an uproar? Wait till the *Heavenly Host* hears about this! *Then* you'll have an uproar on your hands!"

"Really, Gabriel," He said, "There's no reason to get excited. Besides...the Heavenly Host may not even hear about it."

"Why not?" I yelled.

"Because there may not *be* any Heavenly Host in a little while," He intoned somberly. Suddenly the world went dark, and I knew the end had come.

"Well, *that's that*," The Lord said, matter of factly.

"The lights went out!" I shouted. "Now we'll never know how it came out!"

"Never mind that," The Lord said. "Where was Moses when the lights went out?" He asked no one in particular. Just as suddenly, the lights went on again. I realized that The Lord had just been having one of His favorite jokes.

CHAPTER TWENTY-FOUR

The Pan-Angelic Conference

As soon as we entered the hotel, The Lord didn't waste any time engaging the caterers and the banquet room for the *Pan-Angelic Conference.* By the time we arrived at our suite, the atmosphere was shimmering with appearances — mostly Saint Buddha and His Bodhisattvas.

Since The Lord and Saint Buddha were not on speaking terms at that time — which was not unusual in their relationship — all communication between them was addressed to and through me.

"What's Hizzoner up to *now?*" Saint Buddha quipped.

"Tell the old fat buzzard that He'll find out soon enough." The Lord responded loftily.

"I bet it's one of those *crackerjack emergencies,*" Buddha snickered drily.

"Poo on you!" said The Lord.

"Poo on *me?*" the Buddha angrily retorted. "Oh, yeah? Well, *double poo* on *you!*" He screamed in rage.

After the usual round of after-dinner speeches in which everyone praised everyone else, The Lord rose and began to address the multitude.

"Well, gentlemen," He said to the assembly of

archangels, angels, recording angels, and celestial business managers, "we seem to be in an emergency situation..."

"Gentlemen?" shouted Saint Sabrina. "What about us ladies?"

"In Christ is neither male nor female!" rebuffed Ariel.

"Oh, fudge!" yelled Raphael. "Who says Christ is God?"

"Drat!" The Lord moaned. "All we need now is a theological argument. We won't be able to get a Word in edgewise for hours with *this* going on." And so, tossing a thunderbolt over His shoulder to express His displeasure, He left with Archangel Mike and myself to catch the cabaret show downstairs.

CHAPTER TWENTY-FIVE

Return Of The Lord

When we got back, The Lord asked Harab-Serapel if the Trinity Question had been settled.

"Hours ago," Harab replied. "We've been getting up a coffee and doughnut committee since you left, Lord."

"Fine," said The Lord. "Would you mind filling me in on the details?"

"Not at all, Lord," said Serapel. "As you know, the basic problem of the Trinity Question is whether there can be a unified yet multiple being who can remain Absolute and at the same time localize in space as a specific manifestation..."

"No, no, no, you blockhead!" The Lord shouted. "You think I give a prune-whip about the Trinity Question? What happened with the coffee and doughnuts?"

At long last, after the coffee and doughnut question was resolved, The Lord was able to continue His speech.

"You probably have all heard the rumors about what this is all about, and I want to just squelch those rumors right now. This has nothing to do with anything you might have heard about what might be going on between me and Saint Isadora!"

"Nobody knew anything about it until now, hot stuff!"

wailed Saint Isadora, fainting into the arms of Vohu Manah, who lowered her to the floor and took her, right there in front of God and everybody.

"Please let me talk," The Lord shouted above the resulting commotion. "This is serious!"

"Oh, no!" cackled Hashmal. "It's another *crackerjack emergency!*"

"Ahh, shut up!" retorted Hashul, another of the Hayyoth. "Let The Lord talk!"

"Both of you clam up, or I'll knock some heads together!" said Shoftiel.

"You and what army?" razzed Hashmul.

"Infidels and Creeps!" roared The Lord. *"You're gosh-all-hemlock right this is a crackerjack emergency, and you're in it up to your eyeballs!"*

There was a sudden silence.

"I got a good mind to demolish the whole thing," The Lord confided in a whisper. The comment was louder than he realized, and elicited some response.

"You been saying 'This Is The End' every couple thousand years now, Lord!" added Lamediel, who had his *own* reasons for wanting to ring down the curtain.

"Well?" shouted The Lord. "Haven't I delivered?"

"Yeah," reluctantly agreed Haniel of the Tarshishim, "But it wasn't like we expected."

"This is it," The Lord pronounced. "The End. All because of these humans."

"You mean we got into a mess on account of a few idiots here on the planet Earth?" asked Archangel Umahel.

"A few *billion* idiots," corrected Nachmiel.

"So I underestimated," he snapped. "But you don't mean to say that this crummy little planet is going to get in the way of the whole program? Why don't we just blow it up and get it out of the way?"

"Look," said The Lord, "My son *likes* this little planet, and if He likes this planet, it stays, idiots and all! We are going to try to clean it up for Him, *if it takes us till doomsday!"* He asserted, bringing up that rather discouraging subject again for the benefit of the recording and administrative angels.

"Just because the Kid was famous as a Rabbi here, he likes the place so much!" snorted one of the angels in the back.

"Take down that guy's name," The Lord grunted to Khamael, who was recording the minutes of the meeting. The Lord continued. "If you had been more on your toes than you have been, none of this would have happened."

"Oh, that's right, Lord," muttered Futiniel, "Blame it on *us."*

"Take down *that* guy's name, *too,"* He told Khamael... Suddenly the whole place went black and someone shouted out that the end had come.

"Ding-dang right!" The Lord yelled. "This is it!"

"Leaping lizards!" a voice rang out in the darkness — it sounded like Hodniel to me — "This is just some more of your fooling around, Lord, so you can say 'Where's Moses?' — We know your dumb jokes!"

The lights came on again and The Lord grinned sheepishly. "What the fudge," He said. "Not every effort can be a crackerjack."

There was an uproar of shouts and groans which lasted for the better part of half an hour. It was as good a first meeting as could be expected, and The Lord left to go to His suite. All in all He was content with the outcome.

"Those are my sons," He said, *"In whom I am well pleased."*

We slept in until noon, when we went downstairs for brunch. We sat with Sachiel and Zadkiel, who paid for the bill. The Lord as usual insisted He was broke, and turned His pockets inside out to prove His point...

CHAPTER TWENTY-SIX

The Second Day

The second day's series of meetings went slightly better at the outset. There were the usual clan squabbles, which were quickly resolved through the use of great quantities of White Light. When the smoke cleared, we found ourselves subjected to a ramblingly incoherent speech by Eisheth Zenunim regarding the disparate creations of *Right Hand* and *Left Hand* Angels.

After the mob quieted down and Larzod and Capitiel were whisked away for treatment of minor lacerations of the pinions, the meeting once again got onto the business at hand, which incidentally the Angelic Host as a body had not yet discovered, due to continual bickering on *points of ordure.*

Many hours were wasted over seating arrangements, since the Shibaz and Abbadonim would not sit next to each other — nor would they sit opposite each other.

The Lord, expecting such a situation to develop, had previously arranged to introduce the problem in committee and then take it to the floor of the convention.

"The Angel Metatron has the podium," said the chairman.

"Holy Moly, so he does," The Lord said in amazement.

"Hey, wiseguy!" shouted Habudiel, "Put that darn podium back!" But it was too late. Metatron had already gotten past the First Sphere with it. From the looks of things, he wasn't coming back until he had perpetrated whatever little practical joke he had contrived for the occasion.

CHAPTER TWENTY-SEVEN

The Lord Explains
Some Of The Problem

On the third day of the Conference, The Lord took the podium back, and addressed the angels.

"It may not seem to be an emergency," He began. "It isn't visible yet to ordinary perception, but believe me there is a problem. If it isn't stopped now, we may never be able to act upon it again until the next creation."

"Which may be any moment now," I said under my breath.

"The best way for me to explain all this is to give you the basic underlying factors of the situation, then explain to you the exact problem faced by us and a possible solution to it."

"You mean we're going to have to listen to more of your stories, Lord?" asked Futiniel.

"Until I have given you all the data necessary for your understanding of the present problem, Futiniel...Yes."

The angelic host settled back into their red velvet theater seats, tails tucked in underneath, and wings folded out of the way. We knew from past experience that there was no rushing Him — He was bound and determined to give us *all* the data necessary.

"I want to explain to you the causes of the existence of

humans on Earth.'' The Lord began.

"As you know, in the cycle of life on the planetary surface every form of life must sooner or later be somehow dissolved into its primary elements of composition.

"On the lower levels this is accomplished through bacteria and microbes which break down the body into small particles of basic matter which are then able to reform into new materials for later generations — not necessarily the same forms as before.

"This is all very well on the bottom of the life chain, but on the top...It was completely different.

"There were several species already contending for the 'top-of-the-line-disrupter-of-other-life-forms.' Indeed some species of lizard, in particular the dinosaurs, seemed promising in this respect.

"However, much as I tried to anticipate this need, the chain of life on this planet reached a limit beyond which it was not able to go.

"That is to say, there was no single plant or animal which could function not only as everyone else's natural enemy, but as its own natural enemy as well.

"This of course led to the discovery of humans and their placement on this planet for the purpose of active transformation of all life forms into that all-important new organic material.

"At first humans were not willing to terminate the existence of all life forms. But after a small operation in which the existing organ of conscience had atrophied and the Third Brain of the Thinking Center had been added for purposes of self-justification, humans were finally able to terminate the existence of all species including their own without even a twinge of regret or Essence-suffering.

"And although they would not under any circumstances like to think of themselves as nothing more than rubbery tubes on legs for the objective purpose of providing fertilizer from food and air, this is exactly what they are and nothing more.

"*Nothing* more, Lord?" asked one of the Sufi Guides.

"Well, perhaps there *is* another function they provide in their existence but it is only secondary to their primary function.

"Ordinarily water would travel by itself through the process of rising and falling. But occasionally this process fails to occur in nature, and humans then have the objective task of absorbing the water into their bodies, later releasing it into the atmosphere through the various processes of releasing superfluous liquids given to them. Thus they are in this respect similar to what they call 'buckets'.

"But even then it was not sufficient to have them only occasionally terminate the existence of other organisms in their continual search for, as they call it, 'food'.

"I mean, if they were to only destroy the planetary bodies of food organisms just for the purpose of their self-pleasure there would not have been enough new organic material for the formation of future generations of organic life. And so a new, even more powerful, impulse was necessary.

"You should know that interplanetary tensions resulting from communication between the large beings called by humans 'Planets', cause simultaneously within human beings the urge to without pause for reflection destroy all organic — and even some inorganic — forms. That is to say, they cannot endure even for a fraction of a second a state of mild agitation.

"Along with this exists the belief that the reason for their discomfort could not possibly be proceeding from 'interplanetary tensions', but that they must have originated from objects and organisms nearby.

"And so, they begin to destroy at these periodic times of interplanetary tension even those organisms not intended by them for the transformation into the results of 'food'.

"In short there is engendered within them the sudden powerful impulse to calm themselves at any cost and as soon as possible. To avoid forever this inner sensation, they would pay anything — if they could but remain forever calm and contented, just like one of their 'milk-producing beings'.

"After the unfortunate disappearance of the Continent Atlantis, Human-Results-of-the-Action-of-Periodic-Planetary -Tension, or as they say, 'war', has occurred on a large scale somewhere among them every single of their years except three...Without such periodic destruction of organic population, there would still remain on the Earth the older outmoded species, such as Saber-toothed tigers, elephants, whales, dolphins, tortoises, and many other species which have become definitely, permanently obsolete.

"Because of this wonderfully predictable nature of theirs, a great deal of otherwise crystallized organic material has been released and is available for new forms of life.

"I should now mention a new form of organic self-destruction invented by these now quite madcap human beings of the planet Earth. They are quite impressed with the concept of 'efficiency'. This idea has very thoroughly taken their fancy in regard to nearly every aspect of their lives. What you may not know about them in regard to this concept is that they equate efficiency directly with the idea of no discomfort and no effort.

"As a result, they continually invent *labor-saving devices* for the purpose of avoiding effort or discomfort of any kind, no matter how slight.

"Because of these inventions of theirs they have gradually included labor-saving devices for the preparation and storage of their foods...which now come to them already prepared and packaged in such a way that they need only pop them into the oven and...if they do not forget to turn it on...they receive the heated food as if it were real food prepared from basic ingredients.

"Due to the necessity now inherent in their psyches in regard to accumulating the medium of exchange representing their labors in relation to each other and also to the

planet — that is to say, 'cold cash' — their food manufacturers feel that they cannot afford waste in the storage or
in the preparation of these foods.

"This feeling may or may not be shared by those receiving
the foods thus prepared and packaged, but since they have
never complained about anything, lest they lose their only
source of food which has been prepared without their direct
participation and effort, the manufacturers and sellers of
these prepared foods have never needed to alter their
methods.

"Because there is so much food to prepare — millions and
even billions of tons daily — no one can possibly find all the
materials which have accidentally found their way into the
said food substances.

"Everyone recognizes — and accepts — the inevitability
of that. It would simply not be possible to locate every bit of
alien matter included by accident in the handling and
processing of such large amounts of food.

"And as a result of this factor, they have what are called
'minimum-worm-counts' for their sauces and juices...And in
this famous 'worm count' of theirs they allow only a certain
'relatively minor' percentage of contamination to accumulate
in these processed foods. But...should the total exceed that
amount regulated by very intelligent and in all cases
objectively beneficent and moral government agencies...the
manufacturer is asked to be more careful next time!

"And in the processing of their meat products they also
have a similar 'count', but instead of counting worms and
bugs they count parts of rodents and rodent hairs, which
have in some way — no one knows how — accumulated in
the meat during processing and packaging, and should the
quantity of rodent meat and hair exceed the amount set by
the bureau of standards...once again the processor is told to
be more careful next time!

"Then the label goes on the product and it is kept in

storage at the factory. Then, when the demand goes up, it is shipped to the jobber...where it is kept in storage. And then it is shipped to the wholesaler...where it is kept in storage. Then — and only then — is it finally shipped to the retailer, where it is kept in storage in back of the store until it is taken to the shelves to replace stock...where it remains in storage until it is sold. Then it goes to someone's home where it is placed on a shelf...in storage.

"Of course during all this time it would be very unprofitable should these foods begin to appear spoiled. Naturally, the food is already quite 'gone'...but the manufacturers — in order to protect their investments — have added 'a little something' to prevent the food from appearing rotten.

"The additives placed in the said food to disguise rot have the extra advantage of being 'cancer causing', thus increasing the number of victims by at least four times.

"And so you can see that in this respect also, humans have increased the efficiency of their objective task of ridding the planet of all obsolete life forms, including their own, which is the reason I called this meeting. On the Planning Board I have another — even more effective — organic life form not requiring all the ersatz improvements up until now forced upon these unfortunate humans of the planet Earth, and also capable of self-development.

"I would introduce this new species now, except that humans might very well destroy this new species before it can establish itself. After a few generations it will be quite able to defend itself against anything. But at first it will be extremely vulnerable.

"I had hoped that humans would exterminate themselves without our help.

"There is a time limit, because although the need for termination of all obsolete species is always present, I *had* planned on the continued existence of the planet itself.

"We can only pray that humans will discover a new and deadly method of self-extermination before they decide to use their nuclear weapons for the same purpose.

"There is still however, some hope even for this small contribution to the elimination of humans on the planet Earth...And that is a new, for them, method of eating in which rather than serving foods one course at a time, thus allowing a suitable period for the body to process the said food, and allowing the device used by the organism to signify that the state of organic satisfaction has been reached and that no further food intake is necessary to turn off the 'hunger drive', they serve everything all at once on a large plate, and devour the entire meal before the appestat can possibly begin to operate. Thus they take in more than the organism is able to process, leaving food to decompose inside the body. This produces the result that poisons remain within the organism.

"The organic material not consumed and processed as food certainly classifies as a poison...Since it has not been processed and thus altered into organic feeding substances for the smaller parts of the body, it remains as food, just as it was when it entered the organism.

"And in this state it is subjected to warm temperatures... Very warm indeed. Warm enough to make the food into extremely suitable food for bacterial agents, thus beginning the stage in which the said substance shows results of bacterial interest.

"After it begins to rot — and only afterward — is it recognized as 'poison' by the organism and transformed into a substance which can be carried out of the body by the blood, and by the saline solution called by humans 'sweat'.

"This could possibly increase the number of victims of contemporary agricultural business combines, but not possibly enough to account for the ever-growing population. And there are as well some stubborn human beings who eat only those foods which do not destroy the organism, and moreover, eat them in such a way that they actually contribute to the well being of the organic form. How are these stubborn individualists going to be eliminated?

"There must be some solution to this dilemma...And we must find it quickly before time runs out and the planet is destroyed.

"We haven't got much time left, either...Very soon now another period of *Koriensus* is going to occur. If they don't destroy the planet along with themselves during the next period of *Koriensus*, it will be a miracle...In a manner of speaking.

"There are some possibilities..."

"For instance, there now exists the potential for deliberate or accidental epidemics resulting from experiments with bacteria and viruses being conducted in some of their research centers.

"And in still other research centers of theirs experiments are proceeding now which, deliberately or accidentally could cause radical variations in body formation, or as they say, *mutation.*

"And there is further hope...Over a long period of time there has grown among these humans the habit of fearing the inevitable process of their future absolutely certain planetary death.

"They have taken all possible steps to insure that no reminder of this future certainty could in any way occur in their presences, by isolating all immediate candidates for the next world in special communities — what are called 'rest homes'.

"Along with the isolation of these communal elders, they also isolated in educational institutions the younger generation from middle and later generations. In this way each generation is forced to exist separated from any possible All Embracing Compassion And Understanding Flowing From Grandfather To Father To Son, and likewise from Grandmother To Mother To Daughter, for which idea they of course have no contemporarily existing word.

"As a possible result of isolating generations it is guaranteed that no knowledge from previous generations will survive.

"In this way the mistakes of the past generations of humans will be repeated, hopefully on a much larger scale than ever before.

"Thus it may be possible to introduce entirely new weapons...New to them of course, but not at all new to past generations of humans...which can be used only against human forms and which have no effect whatever on other forms of life.

"It is fortunate that they have not received knowledge of the previous existence of this same super-bomb, forgotten due to wars and revolutions and the aforementioned isolation of generations.

"If they did have access to such information they might *not* construct these 'new and improved' weapons and super-weapons...But I doubt it.

"Even more hopeful as a result of this is the growing helplessness of young beings arising in new generations. If this continues...and should there be a shortage of processed foods and other necessary items...They will not survive for very long.

"This isolation of generations has produced a new and delightfully ignorant breed of youngsters...Who believe that when they open a can of something or other — nobody knows just what — and place it in a pan to 'cook' for one hour or so, they have 'made something'.

"But if you asked one of these 'mama's darlings' to tell you exactly what was *inside* one of these 'somethings', they could not tell you very much unless they read the label, and even then they might not be able to pronounce most of the words...

"It is possible that we will not have to take any direct action at all, thanks to all these factors..." He told the assembly.

"But on the other hand, what if these things do not take place as anticipated? What then? What if these humans should happen — against all odds — to survive the next impending period of *Koriensus*?

"But this is only part of the problem...I will continue my explanations tomorrow at the same time," He announced, giving the signal to His vendors to begin selling programs, popcorn and soft drinks.

CHAPTER TWENTY-EIGHT

The Fourth Day Of
The Pan-Angelic Conference

We assembled as usual in the narrow lecture hall upstairs. The Lord was a little late, but it gave us all time to share the latest gossip.

He walked in, accompanied by His bodyguards. By this time He needed them, because He could not move ten steps in any direction without becoming besieged by lobbyists.

"Tell us, Lord," queried Fakr Ed-Din, after the hall quieted down, "why do we always have to bail these humans out of trouble? Why can't they stop their destructive behavior by just *deciding* to, as all other beings in the universe are able to?"

"Humans cannot do anything," the Lord replied. "They at one time could exercise free will, but no longer.

"I can illustrate this by telling you about two fellows existing on this planet. Two men who were outwardly different, but inside completely the same. Yet, to humans, these two men represent conscious and sane individuals quite capable of living exemplary lives.

"The first, Mr. Ajabar, was thin and pale, with restless eyes which darted this way and that. He continually made nervous movements with his body, like those of a sparrow.

He spoke rapidly, as if afraid someone would stop him before he got his idea all the way out.

"He gestured wildly as he spoke, giving all his words the emphasis he believed they deserved. But of course for this terribly important and busy man, *everything* he said and did had extreme importance.

"With only this little sample of data regarding his manifestations, one still ought to be able to determine that he was 'a twitchy-bird'.

"The second man, Mr. Hushig, seemed as different as possible from his neighbor. He was stout, dark, and ponderous. He had a sort of musing, dreamy quality, and his face was placid and relaxed.

"He often fell into states of deep abstraction, rarely becoming excited about anything. He was always sure that there was sufficient time to accomplish anything that really needed doing.

"At Mr. Ajabar's home, as soon as the breakfast was on the table he could be seated and halfway finished with the meal, having already dressed, shaved, and paced up and down for several hours.

"If his understanding and loving wife did not follow in his footsteps — while still warm — then he would pour his own coffee — which is a dark liquid made of something or other, nobody knows just what — and be halfway out the door while the rest of his family were just getting ready to sit down at the table.

"I'm in a desperate rush this morning," he would say. "There might be a customer waiting at the shop when I open! Can't you have breakfast ready any earlier than this?"

"Before the others had taken the first bite of breakfast, he would be out the door and on the way to his place of business. And yet he continually wondered that he was plagued with dyspepsia.

"But on the other hand, Mr. Hushig went about his business on an entirely different basis. He was in no hurry to go to bed at night, so why should he be in a hurry to wake up?

"Breakfast is ready," His wife would gently tell him as he lay in bed, eyes closed and body fully relaxed.

"Is it on the table?" he would ask her.

"It will be in a moment," she would answer.

"Wake me when it's actually on the table," he would reply. And then he would compose himself for his morning reverie, which often unavoidably developed into another little nap.

"But dear," she would urge him, "The sun already has been in the sky for over an hour. You might miss some customers at the shop."

"Yes, yes," he would say. "I'll get up soon. There's time enough. After all, the world wasn't made in a day."

"Now *there's* where he was wrong. I knew I should never have allowed the Publicity Department to make up that pamphlet.

"But as I was saying — when the breakfast bell would ring at Mr. Hushig's house, he would still be in bed, deep in thought.

"There's the bell!" he would exclaim, jumping out of bed. "I didn't think it was that late!" And he would run downstairs to find that everyone had already finished eating. He would drink his cold coffee and eat his cold eggs, grumbling just a little.

"It usually happened that Mr. Ajabar got to his store a full hour before anyone showed up, and he would pace back and forth in despair, thinking that he might have to go into forced bankruptcy by noon if no customers came to buy things from him that morning.

"On the other hand, Mr. Hushig would arrive an hour or two after the opening time stated on the card above the door knob, feeling that if anyone were truly interested in his merchandise, they would eventually return for it.

"One day Mr. Ajabar decided to go on a vacation to the city *Meshkintzor*. He mentioned this little trip of his to his friend Mr. Hushig, who asked, very naturally, in which direction he would be going.

"By the North Road," he replied.

"As far north as Ishutiun?"

"Yes, I was thinking of stopping there overnight."

"How long will you be gone?" his friend inquired.

"Two weeks." said Mr. Ajabar.

"That's not long enough to see everything," his friend told him.

"I can see a great deal in a very short time," said Mr. Ajabar. "But in any case I cannot spare more time away from my business."

"How long will you stay in the city?" asked Mr. Hushig.

"Six days in all," he said.

"The upshot of this was that they agreed to leave together to go to the city.

"Mr. Hushig thought that the second week in August would be early enough, but his neighbor had planned to leave by the middle of July.

"That is too soon, my friend," objected Mr. Hushig. "I wouldn't think of leaving before the second week in August."

"The second week in August?" said Mr. Ajabar. "Oh, no. I must be home long before that. Later in the season thousands of tourists will be milling everywhere, destroying for us quiet and peaceful visitors the calm solitude we enjoy."

"But Mr. Hushig refused to leave as early as the middle of July. And so after many words on the subject they agreed to leave together on the first of August.

"The last week in July came and in six more days the day for beginning the journey would arrive.

"Well! Next Monday we shall start for the city!" said Mr. Ajabar to Mr. Hushig when they met on the street that day.

"Next Monday? You are a little ahead of time, aren't you?" was the cool and passive response.

"Ahead of time?" exploded Mr. Ajabar. "Don't you realize that next Monday is the First of August?"

"Really? How time flies when you're having fun."

"Certainly it's the First...The day on which it has long been understood that we were to leave on our Summer vacations."

"Yes, but I did not understand that we were to leave on the *very* first of August."

"Not on the very first? Not on the very first?" yelled Mr. Ajabar, jumping up and down in rage. Then what *did* you understand? Doesn't the First of August *mean* the First of August?"

"Oh, of course it does. But when we speak of the 'First' of a coming month, we generally mean the early portion of it, don't we?"

"Not me," snapped Mr. Ajabar.

"Well, to me it means the early part of the month," said Mr. Hushig.

"Then you don't intend to leave on Monday?" asked Mr. Ajabar.

"That's right," said Mr. Hushig.

"Then when will you be willing to start?"

"On Wednesday."

"But I've already made up my mind to go on Monday," said Mr. Ajabar, "And once I've made up my mind to do something, I don't like to change it."

"Now, now, my friend," said Mr. Hushig, "This is being too particular."

"A week passed quickly, with Mr. Hushig scarcely giving a thought to his journey and the preparation necessary for it.

"There will be time enough for all that on Monday and Tuesday," he thought to himself.

"Aren't you supposed to leave on Wednesday?" his wife asked him when he was leaving for work on Saturday morning.

"Yes, of course," he replied.

"And aren't those your best boots?" she asked, glancing at his feet.

"Yes, they are," he said.

"Then you'd better get them fixed," she said, "Because you'll be walking a great deal, and if you try to go sightseeing in those you'll hurt your feet."

"All right," he agreed, and started to go to work.

"It was his intention to go to the shoe repair shop directly after he left the house, but as the shop was not on the way to his place of business, he concluded that it would be just as good to stop there on the way back from the shop at lunchtime.

"Did you get your boots fixed?" his wife asked him as he came into the house for lunch. She knew his habits, and was always on the watch for such things.

"No, I completely forgot all about it," he admitted.

"Well, take them with you and wear your old ones," she said. "Then you can drop them off and pick them up on Monday."

"I'll try to remember this time," he told her.

"Ten to one you never think about your boots again until I remind you about them at supper tonight," she said.

"Mr. Hushig was quite amused at this remark.

"What about the boots?" asked Mrs. Hushig as they sat down to dinner that evening.

"Well, I'll be tweedled!" he shouted in shock and surprise.

"You didn't drop them off at the shoe repair shop?"

"No — I completely forgot about it."

"I thought this might happen," she said, "You won't be able to leave on Wednesday, of course."

"Oh, no? After supper I'll go over to his house and give the boots to him so he can bring them into his shop first thing Monday morning."

"Aren't you going to bring those boots over to Mr. Tanner's house tonight?" she asked him later that evening as he sat cozily in his large cushioned chair, reading the paper.

"Oh, not tonight," he replied. "It's Saturday, and there's no sense going over there now. He won't work on Sunday anyway, and I can just go over first thing Monday and give them to him. He'll still have two days to work on them."

His wife just smiled and shook her head.

"Why are you smiling?" he asked her. "Don't you see as well as I do that nothing can be done about it tonight? Why should I run over there tonight when I can accomplish the same thing Monday morning?"

"She did not reply to this, so he returned to his reading.

"Of course on Monday Mr. Hushig had once again forgotten to stop at the shoe repair shop on his way to work. At ten o'clock he suddenly remembered, and started off to see the shoe repair man.

"How soon can you have them ready?" he asked.

"First thing Saturday morning," was the answer.

"Saturday? I have to have them by tomorrow night!"

"Can't do it," said Mr. Tanner.

"Don't tell me that. I have to have them."

"Why didn't you bring them in sooner?"

"After a little persuasion the shoe repairman agreed to exert himself in order to complete the repair by Tuesday night. Satisfied with this promise, Mr. Hushig worried no more about it.

"Morning came and the boots arrived. He started out to look for a cab, but the taxis that were usually in their stands half an hour earlier had gone with the morning traffic.

"He walked to the main street, where a cab could sometimes be hailed. Finally at eight-thirty he found a cab but didn't get back to the house until ten minutes of nine, too late to get the baggage and catch the train which Mr. Ajabar had already boarded.

"Very early Wednesday morning Mr. Ajabar had risen and dressed. He didn't have to pack, because everything had been already packed by Monday night, and the suitcases had remained by the door downstairs since then.

"But at five A.M. breakfast hadn't even been started. And so when he met the cook on the stairs, he confronted her with more than just a little anger.

"Please get the breakfast on the table," he said. "I'm leaving for the city at nine this morning."

"But the cook never liked to be hurried and reacted by slowing down even more. As it happened breakfast was on the table by six, the usual time. Even then, he poured the scalding hot coffee down his gullet a full cup at a time, and swallowed his steak, eggs and toast in great mounds of half-chewed mouthfuls.

"He barely noticed them as they went down. He choked down the last bite of his breakfast, long before anyone else had taken three mouthfuls of their food, pushed his chair back with a squeak against the floorboards, and ran down to the front door to look for the taxicab.

"In sudden fear that the cab might not arrive in time, he spent the next few minutes in a state of nervous despair. At eight fifteen the cab had still not yet arrived.

"Just as I figured," he said. "You can't trust anyone these days." He started to walk down the street in order to locate another cab. Just as he turned the corner the cab drove up to his door. Twenty minutes later, Mr. Ajabar returned with another cab.

"By this time he was very excited, and his imagination completely dominated his reason. He could hear nothing the first cab driver said, and amid the confusion and haste the trunk and suitcase were taken to the second cab and off he dashed, yelling at the driver to hurry — and incidentally forgetting in the uproar to kiss his wife and children goodbye.

"After the other passengers had settled down for the journey Mr. Ajabar sat brooding over things. Mr. Hushig had not showed up, and he would have to make the trip by himself. And if Mr. Ajabar had known it would be like this, he could have left two weeks earlier.

"At two in the afternoon he arrived in the city. He quickly grabbed a bite to eat at a fast-food restaurant right next to a very fine restaurant in which he could have eaten much better food for exactly the same price...Had he had the time for it.

Then he started out to see the sights, having sent his baggage over to the hotel. He had a friend who lived in the city, on Taghant Street, to whom he had written earlier, and whom he had promised to visit while he was staying there.

"Ajabar had intended to do just that, but since his stay in the city was so limited, he felt that every moment was valuable and must be used only for the attainment of his aim in seeing everything possible as quickly as possible. It seemed like a terrible waste to go all the way to Taghant Street just to see a friend.

"And so without having any particular goal in mind, he began walking as quickly as he could until he reached a park. But although he had passed many beautiful sights all during this rapid walk of his, he remained true to his aim to go as quickly as possible through everything of interest. And from the park he set off on a hunch toward the river to the east of the city.

"He walked quickly through endless rows of tenement houses, industrial buildings, warehouses, factories and fishmarkets. It was sundown by the time he returned to his hotel, suffering from a headache and extreme fatigue.

"As soon as he bolted down his breakfast early the next morning, he sailed out of the hotel to get a better start, and fully determined to have a more satisfactory experience than he had the day before.

"When he arrived at the museum, he saw that there were too many displays to see in the time he had available. In this king of all museums was a collection of paintings, sculpture, and ancient art the like of which did not exist anywhere else.

"Here, an art lover might enjoy himself for months — and even after that time he would not have seen one-tenth the collection. The pleasure which Mr. Ajabar had anticipated was now within his reach. Around him — even though surrounded by many annoying examples of objective art, which did not interest him — were the most exquisite examples of rococo anywhere.

"He was too excited to calmly look at the collections in an orderly way. He began running madly through the museum, glancing over his shoulder at the objects he had passed, moaning that all he could see was a blurred streak of color and form.

"There was a particular painting in that museum to which all the newspapers of the day had often referred, and for which the museum had paid many of their dollars.

"Mr. Ajabar longed to see it, but there was an enormous line of people waiting to see it also. Finally, he came almost to the end of the long wait to see this famous picture, but he happened to glance at his watch. It was almost twelve, and he had not even seen the reservoir yet!

"He darted out of the line and jumped in front of the famous painting, exclaiming as he did so, even before he had seen it, "Ah! Beautiful! Exquisite! Incredible!" and then without pausing for breath, turned and bolted out of the museum and onto the street.

"He stopped a cab and got into it. "The reservoir, and quickly!" he told the driver.

"He had no particular object in seeing the reservoir, beyond simple curiosity and the fact that he had seen so many color advertisements about its wonder and stunning beauty. The cab was making slow progress in the busy traffic.

"Hey," he shouted to the driver, "Are you asleep up there?"

"Of course the driver responded to this by slowing down very ostentatiously, and at every cross-walk stopping for pedestrians even if they were a half block away.

"At last Mr. Ajabar's patience, what there was of it, was

exhausted, and he leaped out of the cab, handing the fare to the driver, saying, "Take your fare! I can walk faster than you can drive!"

"As he got out of the cab, he slammed the door. The driver, now livid with rage, pressed his foot all the way down against the accelerator, and the vehicle flew up the street and was in seconds lost to view.

"His emotional and physical state, combined with the added exertion of walking in the hot sunlight, soon produced perspiration, adding its discomfort to his natural state of inner agitation.

"He strode purposefully onward toward the reservoir, which, he learned, was at least a mile away. He could not bring himself to take another cab — he now hated all cabs, their drivers even more...and he was beginning to look with suspicion at buses also.

"And so, half walking, half running, he got past the shaded sidewalks of the city and into the open lots of the suburbs. He pressed on, sweating and cursing.

"Finally he reached the reservoir just to the degree that he could see the stone steps leading upward, but he was so exhausted that he could not climb them, and just stood there looking up at the wall which towered fifty feet above him...

"Now that he had reached his objective, even if only superficially, he lost all interest in the project.

"Bah! he exclaimed, looking at the big stone wall. Is this what I made myself sick to see?" And turning around he walked back to a cab stand, from which a cab would start every few minutes to go into the city. One had just come into line, and the first was just starting off.

"Hey, you!" he shouted. "Wait for me!" Mr. Ajabar began to run after him, his arms waving wildly and shouting at the top of his voice for the driver to stop. The driver remained oblivious to the commotion behind him.

"He can't hear you," called the driver of the cab just next in line. "But I'm going to start in a few minutes," he added.

"A few minutes?" said Mr. Ajabar in horror. "By then it will be too late! That driver heard me...I know he did." Just as he said this, he noticed that the cab which had pulled away was stopped at the curb a few hundred yards down the street, waiting for a light to change.

"Tired, overheated and angry, he began to shout at the cab to stop, running toward it, shaking his fist, trying to catch it before it could pull away into street traffic again.

"He had gone only a few steps, however, before he tripped and fell to the ground. As he lay there with a sprained ankle, he moaned, "Why does this always have to happen to me?"

"Only a few days after he had left home he returned, unable to walk except with the aid of a crutch. And he remained in that condition for the remainder of his little vacation. At least his family now got to see him for a while, since he could not run about after this and that.

"And what about Mr. Hushig? Do you think he did any better?

"Only on Thursday did Mr. Hushig manage to get out of the house on time to board the train to the city. But since he had waited until the last possible minute to arrive at the station, he had to leap on board the train as it was moving, and his trunk and suitcase remained on the boarding platform.

"Throw me that trunk and suitcase!" he shouted to the porter, who stood there gazing as if both hypnotized and paralyzed. It was all over in a moment. He was on his way to the city without his luggage, which sat on the boarding platform behind him.

The steward promised that the luggage would be found and forwarded to his hotel in the city by the afternoon train.

"About as easy in mind as it was possible to be under the circumstances, he arrived at the city several hours later, and looked for Mr. Ajabar, but he was still having his adventure at the reservoir.

"He ended up by going to the train station waiting for the

afternoon train to arrive with his luggage. When it did arrive, it was a little after ten in the evening. But the luggage was not on board.

"He began to feel hungry, but since it was late, only the better restaurants were open. Without his suit and tie, he could not hope to get in. So he returned to his hotel room, disappointed and hungry.

"The next morning a telegram arrived. "Luggage found — Will send it by afternoon train."

"His luggage arrived that evening, and he spent the rest of the time until he was ready to retire by lounging in the lobby of the hotel.

"The following morning he felt too indisposed to go out looking at the sights. For a man of his habits the vexing anxiety of the past two days had been too severe. He felt feverish, and his nervous system was all jangled up.

"And so after taking some breakfast delivered by room service, he remained in his hotel room all day, watching television and reading the newspaper. And so it went for the remaining part of the two weeks.

"Finally he had to leave and return home.

"How was your vacation, dear?" she asked when he got back.

"Same as always, dear," he said. "Never managed to see anything. That city is just too big to visit for two weeks and expect to see all the sights."

The Lord concluded His talk at that point, and the emcee took over.

"Tonight's the big art auction," he said over the loudspeaker as we walked out of the auditorium into the bar.

"Do you think they understood what I was trying to say?" The Lord asked me as we ordered our drinks.

"I don't know...How did it relate to what you were saying about humans not being able to do anything for themselves?"

"Make it a double," The Lord told the bartender.

CHAPTER TWENTY-NINE

The Fifth Day Of
The Pan-Angelic Conference

The next day The Lord told the assembly of angels that He was going to explain to them the reason why humans were not able to have relationships with anyone or anything, including their planet.

"As it happened, there was an old man of the warring class of upper income inhabitants of the Continent Europe during the period called the *Dark Ages*, which marks for contemporary humans the period between the collapse of the Roman Empire and the 'modern world', living in a castle called *Zamaqirk*," the Lord began.

"He lived in his castle — except during those times when he was out in the lands to the South in order to murder the inhabitants for reasons best known to himself — of course not by himself but with a larger gang.

"His wife had, due to the sudden outbreak of an unknown disease several years earlier, succeeded in leaving the planet for the seven hundred and sixty-six thousand nine hundred and fifty-first time. In short, she died.

"A distant relative of theirs, having no other close relations, had when he died left in the care of this old kinsman of his a beautiful young girl; his only child.

"This young girl, causing in the presences of everyone around her the automatic reaction of affection, perhaps due to her long golden hair, voluptuous figure and large blue eyes — or maybe just because she had dimples — became very quickly the 'pet darling' of the castle, and had by doing nothing other than breathing deeply earned the respect and admiration of the knight's two sons.

"And eventually, as is always the case among humans on Earth, a gradual formation combining the impulses of desire, guilt, affection, greed, envy, jealousy, lust, vanity and the unconscious urge to reproduce oneself began to crystallize in the presence of both these two brothers in regard to the said golden-haired young girl, whose name was at that time 'Angelique', which said formation of impulses is called by humans the emotion 'love'.

"From the first moment the young girl had arrived at the castle, the old man believed that she would naturally marry his oldest son Henry, who was their heir to his estate, name and title, rather than his youngest son, Conrad.

"Even though Henry felt for Angelique a deep and profound love, combined with equally deep and profound sensations centering from time to time in the area below the navel, the girl refused his subtle advances and instead returned the younger son's more obvious passion, expressed aloud with the greatest fanfare possible always and everywhere.

"Henry, even though deeply disappointed, tried to feel nothing but happiness for the two of them and to rejoice in his brother's success. At first the elder brother's distress upset Angelique, but shortly she forgot all about it, and began to notice other things, among which were the impressions she was able to produce on Conrad, the youngest son.

"At about this same time a monk — considered holy because of wounds he had sustained in battles in the land to the South, and also because of his vocal tirades against the

brutish heathens — appeared in the town and began to
arouse interest in the local inhabitants regarding the
prospect of returning with him and giving the inhabitants of
that country 'what-for'.

"Henry, experiencing by now extreme sadness regarding
his brother's love affair, but not at all feeling envy toward
him, could not be a continual witness to it, and so he
announced that he would answer the call of the holy monk.

"But Conrad was also stirred by the impulse to go into
battle. However, he felt only the longing for action and
excitement, and became completely dominated by the
adventures created in his imagination concerning the war
and his own imagined heroic part in it.

"The tears of the young Angelique and the supplications
of the old man were entirely useless.

"Who will remain at the family seat held for centuries by
our forebears if you both abandon it now, perhaps never to
return?" he said.

"Then suddenly a great feeling of remorse came over
Henry, seeing his once powerful father reduced to tears.

"Even though I feel an urgent desire to leave," he said, "I
will bow to your wishes."

"But Conrad still resolved to seek glory and adventure,
according to the fiery drama proceeding within his
imagination.

"You will have to bear this decision of mine," he told
them. "Plant a sprig of laurel in order to make a hero's
wreath for me when I return in triumph."

"The very next day the young knight set off for his
adventure. At first, Angelique seemed unable to be consoled
in her grief. But once again the action of the psyche came
into play, and her love began to drop off to sleep like a tired
baby.

"And upon awakening from this drowsy state several
weeks later, she began to feel indignant and outraged at the
treatment she had received from Conrad.

"Every day she heard the complaining whispers of her inner self, and one day weeks later she was suddenly seized with a peculiar sensation not unlike those manifestations common to 'Saint Vitus' Dance'.

"She now began to notice more and more the proud youth Henry, who had been forced to live under the same roof with his rejected love and still managed to remain true to his brother.

"She suddenly began to admire all his good qualities which had somehow escaped her attention before.

"Even though Henry was not unaware of the change in her affections, he proudly refused every impulse arising in him regarding her love for him, for the sake of his brother, Conrad.

"The old knight was greatly pleased when Angelique came to him one day and amid tears and sobbing, disclosed to him this secret of her heart.

"The old knight began to see in his dreams the vision of Angelique sitting in a rocking chair and rocking her baby to sleep, just as his dead wife had done — of course only prior to her death.

"Then he would suddenly remember his younger son fighting for his life in the Southern land, and he would awaken with a start, feeling remorse and grief.

"And because of this grief, and feelings of guilt, he caused a beautiful castle to be built opposite to his ancestral hall, which he intended for his younger son, who would otherwise, according to the laws at that time, have inherited nothing.

"The castle had been completed only one week before the old man passed away. The war in the south was at that same time over. Some of the knights returned, bringing with them the news that Conrad had married a beautiful southern woman during the war, and was now bringing her home with him.

"Henry was enraged to the point of madness on hearing this news. Such dishonorable conduct seemed impossible to him. He went to Angelique and told her, as there was no one else to give her this news. Her face paled and her lips moved a little, but she could not speak.

"One day while standing in the tower overlooking the river, as she did now every day reflecting on her unfortunate destiny, she saw a ship, and called to Henry to come to the tower.

"Suddenly she cried out, and threw herself into the arms of the older brother. There on the deck of the ship stood Conrad in his shining armor, and clinging to his arm was a young woman of the South. Up to now, Angelique had not quite believed the stories.

"As the ship touched shore, Conrad sprang out onto the soil. One of the servants of the castle came to him and told him that the new castle was intended for him by his father.

"Conrad sent word that he and his bride had arrived, but Henry answered that he would wait for him on the bridge between the two castles with sword in hand to kill the faithless brother who had deserted his betrothed.

"They were both equally strong and courageous and their swords clanged away at each other, one in anger and the other in pride.

"Suddenly Angelique burst out from the bushes and darted between them, thrusting them apart from each other.

"She for whom you have drawn your swords is now going to take the veil of the nun and will pray to God — that's me — to forgive you, Conrad, for your falseness."

"Well, I would have liked to help, but what with all my other problems...The effect was that both brothers threw down their swords, and Conrad stood with his head bowed, covering his face with his hands. He did not dare look at the maiden who stood there, a silent reproach to his faithlessness.

"You don't know what it was like out there..." He explained.

"Come, sister," said Henry taking her hand, "This does

not deserve your suffering and tears.'' They disappeared into the ancestral home, Conrad silently gazing after them. A feeling which he hadn't known before rose up in him, and he wept bitterly, feeling for the first time the impulse of remorse.

"The Cloister in which Angelique took her vows and within which she lived and eventually found inner peace lay in a valley only a short distance from the two castles.

"A wall was built between the two forts, a silent witness to the feelings between the brothers. Banquets and dances followed one another in the new castle, and the beautiful young southern girl won the admiration of all the knights of the realm.

"But in the castle inhabited by the older brother, grief seemed to take full possession of everything and everyone.

"On the day before Christmas, one year after she had entered the Nunnery, Henry, already quite worn with suffering to the extreme degree, left the castle walls and tottered out onto the park grounds, keeping to the pathway because of his infirmity, and sat down upon a bench kept there for the purpose of pondering and resting.

"And as it happened, this was the same bench upon which Angelique used to sit while waiting for the return of Conrad. As Henry sat there automatically observing the actions of objects and animals in the surrounding space, by automatic association of ideas, this bench began to provoke in him certain memories of Angelique.

"And how although she walked beautifully and proudly before the news of Conrad's infidelity, she became stooped and apparently old, afterward, having to walk with the aid of a cane.

"Henry also recalled the strange friendship that formed between the two women — Angelique, and the Southern woman, in spite of the enmity of the two brothers.

"And he remembered the remarkable circumstances under which these two women met at this bench every day since the day of the battle between the brothers.

"And he recalled how the two women would sit with one another on this bench, and despite the fact that neither spoke the other's language, they would tell each other those things most important to their inner lives.

"Due to this continual deep interchange which took place between them during the six months before Angelique entered the Nunnery, a peculiar kind of language developed between them, consisting of at least two verbal and several sign languages.

"Henry's memories hung in the balance around the two women as the center of gravity of his feelings of nostalgia and suffering.

"His suffering was caused by the knowledge that simply by expressing to Angelique his feelings of love she would be happy to become his wife.

"Even though he knew that he might be the only person on Earth who could cure her illness caused by deep mental and emotional anguish, he could not do this, due to his own weakened state and emotional illness.

"And so he began at that time to construct with his own hands a beautiful cloistered walkway completely around the castle walls.

"And when he had completed it, he sat there on the same bench, contemplating this enormous labor of his on behalf of his love and feelings of remorse for Angelique.

"He noticed after a while of pondering that this effort had only become possible through the suffering he felt for another.

"He passed away on the same day that the bells were tolling for the passing of Angelique. They were carried together in State through the Cloisters made by Henry in memory of his beloved Angelique, and they were buried together in the family crypt.

"Both castles have since fallen into ruin, but the Cloister stands firm to this day, having been built with love and intense effort, and is the scene of many pilgrimages."

CHAPTER THIRTY

The Sixth Day Of
The Pan-Angelic Conference

The next day the Lord explained why humans existing on the planet Earth could not possibly formulate real aim, which question was provoked by several members of the forum gathered in the auditorium.

"I happened to wander once into a shop which displayed through its glass frontage several fascinating carpets, which, because of their rare examples of understanding of Objective Art not emanating from the subjective emotional part of their creators, caught my eye.

"The shopkeeper greeted me with a strange expression obviously mechanical and automatic with him for the purpose of meeting with customers, the result of which — had I not been onmipotent — would have made me feel instantly somehow guilty and at fault for some unknown trespass.

"Why are you here?" he asked.

"I want that carpet," I replied, indicating one of the carpets in the window.

"You wish to buy that carpet only because it is displayed in the window," he said. "Perhaps you believe it is a good carpet because it is displayed in a special way, and that because of this it has a special value." His tone was sarcastic in the extreme as he said this.

"It is only an ordinary carpet," he continued. "There may be thousands exactly like it."

"That is not the reason I am interested in that carpet," I replied. "It reminds me of something."

"Of what?" he asked, suddenly cunning and interested.

"Of the beard of Saint Buddha," I said. From then on his attitude changed markedly.

"You are obviously a possessor of extraordinary knowledge," he perceived. "You remain with me for a few days and allow me to show you something of human nature."

"Well, I could think of a lot of other better things to do, but I agreed to stay.

"Many things can be learned from observing which carpets people are willing to buy — but! One can learn even more if you observe which carpets I do not sell them, even though they wish more than anything to obtain them. Many people believe they have the right to do anything to a carpet which they purchase. They do not realize that they become maintainers, responsible for the life of that carpet.

"They believe that they have purchased the right to destroy it because they have given money. They do not realize a work of high objective art in the effort of the creator of such a carpet.

"I never sell to anyone who buys only for ego gratification a design containing objective art. The turning of a sale toward inferior merchandise is a very important art for the carpet seller. I will reveal to you now the method of the turning of a sale to inferior merchandise according to the understanding of the buyer."

"So saying, he stopped abruptly, for a middle-aged couple entered the shop at that moment. It was easy for anyone to read the look of expectant greed on their faces, thinking perhaps that they would find something valuable which the seller did not recognize as such.

"The shopkeeper Harkounian flashed a quick, secretive

wink in my direction and turned toward them, assuming a blank ignorant expression which, as soon as the couple noted it and judged him accordingly, brightened them up like cockroaches who have suddenly discovered an unwrapped piece of cake.

"It is amazing to report, but that couple left there with thirty large carpets which they had purchased at what was laughingly called the 'wholesale price' but which was actually ten times the usual 'retail price'.

"Mr. Harkounian continued to demonstrate this technique of turning buyers from Real Art to phony art carpets. He demonstrated the ability to sell anything to anyone, and soon had earned for himself enough to restock the store several times over.

"I was surprised, then, when a shabby looking man came into the shop and asked for an inexpensive carpet to be used as a prayer rug, and Harkounian just about fell over himself to give him an extremely rare and expensive carpet woven with the finest example of Objective Art, asking only that it be cared for properly.

"Do not believe this carpet has no price just because I ask no money for it," Harkounian told the man. "It is very valuable in an Objective way. It has a message inscribed in it which must not be lost to future generations. It is an objective view of the nonfantastic world. Before I give this carpet to you, I must have a promise from you that you definitely understand that the price of this carpet is to care for it and to keep it in perfect condition. Do you agree to this?" he finished importantly with an urgent tone in his voice.

"You crazy old man!" the shabby man retorted. "I don't know what you're talking about! This carpet may be rare, but as far as the objective view of the nonfantastic world — you know nothing of the nonfantastic world. You were obviously told this by another. You have no business asking another to care for this carpet. I won't promise to attach myself to anything! Besides which, this carpet will never reach future generations. Even if it did, there is nothing here worth saving. If you want to give me the carpet I asked for, all right. If not, then don't. It's your decision one way or the other. But don't expect me to treat one carpet any differently than any other. To me, it's all the same." And he turned to leave.

Harkounian, who had been full of cheer over the prospect of giving away something of real value, was visibly shaken. Then, suddenly, something in him broke, and he ran after the man, throwing the shop key to me, shouting, "Take me with you. I will follow you anywhere! You are my teacher! I have found a man of Real Knowledge!" He capered madly after the shabby man who strode down the street.

"Occasionally the shabby man would growl at Harkounian, saying "Get away from me, you madman! What in blazes do you think you are doing following me? Are you crazy?"

"I stood around in that shop for a while not knowing how to properly dispose of it, for the shopkeeper had obviously given it up forever.

"I made a sign that said *Gone Out of Business. Please Loot*, and left the door open, but everyone thought that it was a stunt and refused to empty the shop.

"Finally I locked the shop as tightly as possible, putting bars and chains across the front, and made another sign which read *No Trespassing, Violators will be Shot*! and one which read *Guard Dog On Premises*. The shop was emptied within the hour."

After the podium was cleared and the Lord and a few of us went to the bar, the Lord asked whether we had understood the point of *that* talk.

"Yes, Lord," said St. Mike. "Never give a sucker an even break."

"Give me two doubles and a beer chaser," the Lord said to the bartender as he sat down.

CHAPTER THIRTY-ONE

The Seventh Day Of
The Pan-Angelic Conference

"I can explain why I have been continually forced to interfere in the affairs of humans existing on Earth by telling you what happened in the kingdom of Upper Caledonia as an example," He began. The angelic host settled down in their seats as He talked.

"The Upper Caledonians had a king, but they never called him king, because they were very proud people, and had they been forced to recognize that he was their king, they would have revolted immediately.

"So they called him instead the 'Super-Chief Shamanistic-Leveler-Of-Conditions', but he was affectionately known to many of his people as *Hoot-Khoomy*, which means in their native tongue, 'Compassionate Fraud'.

"Hoot-Khoomy's main occupation as king of the Upper Caledonians was to keep the people working.

"Since the inhabitants of Upper Caledonia were not able to arouse the impulse of *fear of starvation* in themselves and could not believe that they would ever be really hungry, they had hired the king to keep them aroused to the point of necessary labor.

"The king's job was to constantly find new and better

ways to produce the said fear within them, for after a while the psyches of the inhabitants of the kingdom of Upper Caledonia would begin to allow the fear to die down into nothingness through the means of forgetfulness.

"Finally the king had run out of ideas. He knew that if he could not now come up with some solution to this dilemma, the entire population would starve before the next Winter was over — and worse, he would be out of a job.

"So the king hired a mob of headhunters from the rain forest, and granting them permission to hunt heads anywhere but in the town he had thus insured a permanent state of fear in the population, allowing him to just sit and think, without having to invent continually some new work-motivation every few months.

"He promised to the said headhunters a payment of one-third of the harvest each year, which if not sufficient would of course result in hunger for the headhunters, leading to the obvious result that they would look for fresh meat in the towns of Upper Caledonia...which said 'fresh meat' continued in quite healthy condition only as long as the food was produced and payment made as agreed.

"For a number of years this arrangement proved to be quite satisfactory for both groups, but after a while the headhunters forgot the original agreement, due to this same maleficent 'forgetfulness' common to the psyches of humans of the planet Earth, and they began ravaging the towns even though they received their portion of the harvest as stated in the agreement.

"And they did this partly because they had realized that by no longer hunting heads they had lost their tribal identity, and also because it had become very fashionable to display the heads of enemies cunningly, atop poles outside one's hut.

"Also contributing to this need of theirs for more heads to display outside their huts was the new craze of their young ladies to engage in courtship ritual only with those young men who managed to display the most heads outside their huts.

"When they invaded the palace itself and removed through force the heads of the king's favorite cook and ladies-in-waiting, he decided that things had gone far enough.

"Of course he had not forgotten that his own head was at stake, too. His first protective measure was to have a special iron collar made for himself. His second measure was to recall everyone to the palace. But of course this meant that they would lose the crops.

"I happened to be in the neighborhood at the time, and explained to Hoot-Khoomy that I would be happy to work out a solution for him.

"We immediately set up blackboards that explained to the people the genuine being-benefits of increasing the food supply. At the same time showing pictures of the most delicious recipes we could think of...

"We must have overlooked something in the human psyche, however — and I am prepared to admit that it may have been my fault — because immediately after the lecture, the people went back into the palace and ate everything in sight.

"It was at this point that I was forced to invent the Quonset Hut. The actual problem was, as it turned out, that they feared the consequences of the sudden removal of their heads while working outside in the fields.

"Through a series of very patient interviews, I was able to determine that not only were they afraid of the headhunters, but they also had other fears which prevented them from leaving their homes to work in the fields, which said fears were the *real* reason they had not been willing to work in the first place.

"These fears of theirs stemmed from the possibility of what the women would do if given the opportunity, as there was always a plentiful supply of chimpanzees and donkeys available to them, as well as the occasional visit of a traveling peddler. Even more concern was caused among them if a peddler arrived with a number of chimpanzees on a cart pulled by a donkey.

"If only something could be arranged so that the Upper Caledonians would not be constrained to leave their homes while working at their daily labors, they could produce those things necessary for their survival.

"It became immediately apparent to me that what was wanted was a completely indoor arrangement which would satisfy both the familial and the survival needs of the Upper Caledonians.

"It was then a simple matter to arrange the population into family groups. As soon as the Quonset Huts were completed by the headhunters, who were the only available labor force, since the Upper Caledonians were unwilling to leave their homes even for this effort, and whom I was forced to pay in their own currency — which at that time happened to be heads — the Upper Caledonians moved into them, never going away more than a few feet from the women, and keeping them well away from the donkeys.

"At first I was forced to supplement the crop of new foods with wine, *manna* and so forth, but after a while the Upper Caledonians began to grow foods which did not require sunlight, which said food substances are called by them mushrooms.

"Even though this food substance cannot provide the necessary transforming substances and vivifying factors for the cells of the body, they showed no interest in exchanging this diet for something more nutritious which required sunlight for its growth.

"And as a result of ingesting only these spore-grown and horn-resembling-foods, they became, due to their resulting slug-like skin coloring, known as *whities*.

"After having successfully completed these labors of mine which solved for them their living and working conditions, I left for other parts, and Hoot-Khoomy remained to rule over a kingdom which for all practical purposes had vanished from the face of the Earth.

"Eventually, he became bored with ruling a land dotted with thatched roof huts and separated his body and essence by hand through a method called by them 'Solo Russian Roulette'.

"Many years passed, and the headhunters began to take up residence just outside the Quonset Huts. This did not interfere with life inside them, as they had wells to provide their water supply and an endless supply of mushrooms to eat.

"But as a result of this, one could not leave one's Quonset Hut even for a minute to see whether or not it was raining, without losing the storage space ordinarily reserved for the brain.

"It became apparent that it was not safe to leave the huts under any conditions. Now, as soon as the Upper Caledonians learned that *they could not go outside even if they wanted to*, they became angry and frustrated. It is always true among these humans that as long as they can freely have something without suffering, they do not under any circumstances want it, but as soon as it is withheld from them, they immediately want whatever it is, and if they cannot have it when they want it, they become angry, upset, frustrated and in many cases violent.

"And so they dug tunnels from one Quonset Hut to another, and in these underground tunnels they held meetings called by them 'councils' in which they planned to wage war on the headhunters and drive them away or kill them off once and for all.

"At this time our own Archangel Lefkowitz decided to assist them by taking a direct role in their affairs, just as I had done earlier.

"Lefkowitz had been thinking the whole thing over, and thought that he would be able to avert the carnage of war if he could only get the Upper Caledonians and the headhunters together in a meaningful dialogue.

"If you can communicate, you can relate," he told them.

"But when the headhunters and Upper Claedonians got together and began relating, they discovered why they did not like each other and made the only common decision they had ever made together.

"They decided to take Archangel Lefkowitz and run him up the flagpole.

"When the mob reached the palace, where Archangel Lefkowitz had been staying, he realized at once that they were in an ugly mood. This was not a difficult observation, as they carried with them several burning effigies and a rope made into a hangman's noose.

"Archangel Lefkowitz knew that it was no use to try to escape. He bravely stood up to them, holding his arms above his head, fingers extended in what is now known as the 'One-Fingered Victory Sign'.

"Wait!" he commanded. The crowed stopped at the foot of the marble stairs.

"Am I Betraya?" he asked in a commanding and powerful voice, alluding to the mythical reappearance of the king Hoot-Khoomy.

"If you see me die, then I will live forever!" he shouted. "I come to you not as an officer or minister, but as a man!"

"Elephant pucky!" someone in the crowd shouted back.

"I come to bring to you wisdom and knowledge. I offer you freedom!"

"Ah, cherry fudge!" said someone else.

"I come to teach you. I come to help you!" he said. A grumbling sound began to grow in the mob.

"Wait!" he cried. "If I have ruled well, assist me. If not, then do not assist me. Let that be my penalty! Do you see me here before you? Is this space occupied? No Smoking! Tickets, please! Can you see me?"

"As he said these last words, the crowd of Upper

Caledonians and headhunters picked him up and took him into an interior room in the palace, where they crammed him into a 'junkyard compactor' which had been specially redesigned by him so that ten people could be buried in the same coffin, thus saving a family the expense of cemetery real estate when funeral costs were at an all-time high.

"The second decision of that mob, also in keeping with the remarkable thinking processes of that infernal psyche of theirs, was to separate immediately into two factions with Upper Caledonians on the one side, and headhunters on the other.

"The result of this decision of theirs was that each side wished to immediately convert the planetary forms of the other side into something more appropriate for the nourishment of trees and flowers than for conversing, dancing and socializing.

"At that point, also in keeping with that strange system of behavior called by them 'perfectly reasonable and justifiable under the circumstances', they ran for their respective armories and began destroying each others' planetary bodies.

"The supposed purpose of their warfare is, as you already know, to destroy the planetary forms of those not considered fit for survival.

"But as they only send their strongest and most intelligent and most ethical youngsters to war, leaving only those considered physically, psychologically, morally, and intellectually unfit to kill, they continually move on a downspiral course to extinction.

"In order to be considered by them 'fit to kill others' one must pass many tests of endurance, courage, and intelligence. This reveals for all of you assembled here the exact reason for their behavior in relation to each other, toward the planet, and toward our efforts on their behalf."

"Lord," came a shout from the angelic host as a whole, "What happened to the Upper Caledonians?"

"I returned there many years later to see the results of this effort of mine and of Archangel Lefkowitz, but all I saw were a few females of Upper Caledonian descent, in congress with some donkeys. But, after all," He said, "Not every effort..."

"When the screaming began, we herded The Lord out through a back exit.

"Just leave the bottle," He told the bartender later.

CHAPTER THIRTY-TWO

Hot On The Trail

By the end of the third week of the Pan-Angelic Conference, it was becoming apparent that things had begun to stagnate. Nothing could get out of committee, and the coffee and doughnuts had not improved since the first day.

So as we all had long expected Him to do, The Lord announced over our ritual breakfast of *Eggs Benedict* that we were going to leave the conference with as many good angels as we could muster except for that clown Metatron, who had been previously assigned to the role of Ha-Satan, the Chief of Seraphim and Holy Adversary. The zipper on the Ha-Satan suit had gotten stuck, and the Lord wouldn't allow him to break it, since the Lord is very budget-conscious.

As a matter of fact, that's the same exact thing that happened to Saint Lucifer when he tried it on. The zipper got stuck, and he was forced to sit around playing Ha-Satan for ages.

"Boy, was that hades!" Lucifer complained afterwards. "Stuck in that hot suit, sweating my you-know-what off!" He was referred to the Wardrobe Department, but as far as I know nothing ever came of it except a few interdepartmental memos. Personally, I think it's deliberate. How else are they going to get anyone to play the role of Holy Adversary?

We left the hotel with The Lord, Mike and me, Raphael, of course — he would feel paranoid if we left him out of it — a bunch of the Grigori and some of the Steerage Committee, among whom were Shams ed-din, Fakr ed-din, and Khidr Rahman. But the best of the lot were those two heavy-duty angels, Archangels Lefkowitz and Rabinowitz, without whom, believe me, the disaster would have been much worse than it is.

We got into our American Zoot-Suits in order to move freely among civilians. They differ only slightly from the 'Frog Suits' we had worn in France, the 'Wog Suits' we had worn in India, and the 'Hog Suits' we had worn in Poland.

And so we zipped up our 'All-American' disguises of skin, hair, facial expression of apathetic boredom, and of course when going out among Americans, the all-important *Negative Emotion Emitter Devices.*

The Lord was wearing a 'Lucky Lindberg' model. I chose a simple 'Gregory Peck' off the rack. Mike was in an 'F.D.R.' with a wheelchair for added effect. Raphael insisted on the 'Ginger Rogers', but we talked him out of it. Finally he came out of wardrobe in his usual unimaginative 'Gustave Dore's *Portrait of Raphael*'.

The next day we all met to consider a plan of action. We had our meeting over a luncheon of roast pheasant and cornbread.

"There's some bird left over, Gabriel," He said as I sat down at the Archangels' table, which The Lord prefers to sit at since they almost always carry the most ready cash. Our Father is, as everyone knows, a Profound Eater, and He considers Himself quite a gourmet — which only means that He eats more often and orders from the right-hand column rather than the left column with all those confusing names of foods.

"Chew your food very very well." He admonished us as we sat there eating our roast pheasant.

"Why?" asked Adoyahel. Only a rube like him would fall for this one.

"I tell you to chew your food well," The Lord said to Adoyahel as we sat back disgustedly waiting for the rest of it — "So that if you eat too much, you do not barf chunks."

"Thanks for elucidating that question, Lord," said Adoyahel just before he barfed chunks.

"Too bad you didn't hear when I gave that advice before, Adoyahel," He said.

"But Lord," said Nasr ed-din, "Just before this you told us to swallow our food whole if possible."

"That" replied The Lord, "is so that the guys on the other side of your mouth can receive their food intact and not in disgusting premasticated lumps."

"What guys on the other side of our mouths, Lord?" asked Archangel Lefkowitz.

"See what I mean?" The Lord guffawed. "You guys don't know a road-apple from a knish! There's these guys, see? They live on the other side of your mouth! Where do you think all that food goes to?"

"Our stomachs?" weakly hazarded Archangel Rabinowitz.

"Of course not!" stormed The Lord. "You guys don't need to eat, do you?"

"No," said Asmodel.

"Well, don't you see?" said The Lord. "There are lots of beings who just don't have the wherewithal to get their own food, so they depend on you guys to procure it. When it goes through your mouths it drops into the 'world behind the mouth', and the beings there eat it — that is, they eat, if it has not in the meantime been hopelessly destroyed by chewing, thus making it unpalatable. And since you are all wearing suits which give you the characteristics of humans, all your food goes to the 'world behind the mouth' just as it does with them. Have some vanilla discustard pie?" He offered as He finished this discourse. I barfed chunks.

"It all started on *The Day I Noticed That The Clock Wasn't*

Doing Anything,'' The Lord began.

"What did?'' asked Hadriel.

"This mess humans on the planet Earth have gotten us into,'' The Lord replied.

"What mess?'' asked Galadriel.

"I'm getting to that,'' The Lord said. "It was the day after *The Day I Noticed That Nothing Was Happening.*

"I looked at the clock and realized that the hands were not moving. I had been fascinated by this apparatus before, but had not been able to think of a use for it.

"It happened at that time that I was intending to do something — in accordance with my discovery the day before — and that what I intended to do was not exactly a 'six', but it wasn't a 'four' either. And looking at the clock, I began to realize that I could use it as an automatic apparatus to set the occurrence I had in mind at the function of 'five'. And since I was occupied at that moment with other more important matters, I without thinking set the clock between 'four' and 'six' at the number 'five'.

"But suddenly there was a wrenching sensation, and I realized that I had started *time* — and since that very moment at which I started the clock moving again by hand, everything has run downhill. Now whenever the clock says 'three', why, that's what time it is! And whenever it says 'five', it has to be five o'clock.''

The smoke-filled conference room was the result of a little demonstration The Lord had just given a few minutes earlier, and the angels were beginning to drop off to sleep, when The Lord finally got to the point — why everything in the universe had gone wrong, and why humans were at the center of the cause of the situation.

CHAPTER THIRTY-THREE

The Lord's Explanation
Of It All

"Now that I look back on it," said the Lord, "I can see that the destruction of this creation by humans of the planet Earth is as inevitable as apple pie and ice cream."

"Tell us about it, Lord," encouraged Ruphiel. The Lord was obviously trying to get something out — something about what He had done that had caused it all to go wrong — but He was having trouble expressing it.

"I better start at the beginning of this little episode," The Lord began. "I had been at my drawing board for several days, and nothing had gone right. Like this..." He said, holding up a drawing of something that looked like a puffy hippopotomus with feathers, "This was supposed to be a pumpkin — but it's all wrong."

"Looks okay to me, Lord," said Galadriel.

"Yeah, but when *this* was a *pumpkin*, you should have seen the *chickens!*" He said sadly.

"The thing is," The Lord continued, "when you make one thing, the rest of the world around it has to conform to the same laws you set up for that one object. You can't have one object existing in a world which doesn't conform to the natural laws of the planet...That is, you couldn't — until I

[172]

created humans of the planet Earth.''

"Oh, no,'' I groaned inwardly, suddenly understanding what He had done.

"You have to understand why I did it,'' He said in a pleading tone. "You can't know how it was. The same old peanut butter sandwiches day after day, the room continually changing at random intervals, the light on all the time so I couldn't sleep, and nag, nag, nag...''

"I don't understand, Lord...'' said Hadriel. "Why didn't you complain about it?''

"To whom?'' The Lord replied. "I was all alone at the time.''

"Oh...Of course,'' Galadriel said, in some confusion.

"So I went into the Study to try to think,'' said The Lord. "I was wondering how to get to sleep, and I wanted a book or two to read. Then there was the confounded radio blaring all the time in the Other Room.

"As I sat down at my desk, I happened to notice that there was a pencil and paper lying there. I doodled some notes, and then when I had filled the paper completely, I thought to myself — Now, where am I going to get another piece of paper? And then the idea came to me.

"An automatic creator who did not conform to the laws of the universe...'' I said laconically.

"Why, yes — That's exactly what I was going to say. I realized at last why I was having so much trouble. It was because I was forced to do all that creating myself, and it was hard for me. I didn't care what happened with each thing — it was all the same to me. I needed something or someone that *cared*. Someone who could really get *into* each object of creation.

"You think it's easy to create something from nothing, but how would you like to have to figure out every detail with nothing to base it on? What form it was going to have, what mass it would be composed of, what it was supposed to do, what color it would be, what temperature it would maintain, how it would process food, if it ate anything, and most of all, how it would regulate itself.

"That was my biggest hope, finding something that would self-regulate. Up to then I had made all my created objects hollow inside so that they could be operated like hand-puppets, into which I had to fit myself simultaneously to give the impression that each one had a life and intelligence of its own, and its own will and intention. But behind it all, there I was — and it was disappointing in the extreme to have to run everything and know that I was running it all.

"I tried simplifying all action into three basic functions, but the fact is that while this made it possible to step back from the actual operation of the figures, they were still not capable of individual decisions and thought. But at least I didn't have to get inside a bunch of puppets. I could operate them from behind the back.

"I saw that I was too impartial and objective to really create anything specific. What I needed was a professional creator — someone who could create something and think about it and make it work. I needed some good old 'American ingenuity'.

"My answer to this was to create only one thing, which would once and for all solve this dilemma for me. I decided to create a being who would be the ultimate creator.

"I had the idea to create a being that would do nothing but create, and would wish to do nothing but create. I made it so that it would create in a perpetual and endless stream in order to compensate for its own limitations, which were deliberately severe in order to arouse this impulse.

"But my ultimate creator at first made a few particles of matter and then sat around watching the particles, waiting to be amused. I had the sudden realization that in the creation of this perfect and perpetual creator of mine, something had gone definitely wrong.

"I was constrained to add a little something that would

make that reluctant creator into a perpetual creator who did not demand amusement. And so I placed around its Essence the formation of an automatic identity — a false identity of course, since the real one had no interest in anything whatever and was content to simply sit there forever — and I called this false identity which contained compulsive programs to be creative no matter what, and to strive continually for new and better things, the *psyche*."

"Oh, for crying out loud," I muttered under my breath.

"What?" The Lord asked in an impatient tone.

"Nothing, Lord," I replied.

"Now the next question was, where was I going to get the material for all this creation? The substance for creation had to be either in unlimited supply or it had to be recyclable. I decided for reasons of economy on the latter.

"And to give this creator of mine the necessary motivating force for its evolution into a self-conscious and therefore self-regulating and self-initiating being, I decided to enclose it inside the creation substance itself and to make the substance of creation completely *plastique* with its own consciousness so that it could respond with perfect feedback to the creator's creative ideas.

"That meant that the substance of creation could accomodate the creator by becoming whatever the creator could dream up. How was I to know that this creator of mine would begin to have nightmares?

"And I included in the psyche of that creator of mine the impulse *To Continually Strive To Escape*, which even if only partially accomplished, would have the effect of erasing all previously recorded patterns of creation existing within the substance of creation.

"And to make it impossible for the creator to actually escape from the substance of creation I implanted within his psyche the idea that he was clothed by substance and was naked without it. Along with this I placed the fear of exposure, or *Striving To Hide Nakedness*, which is today known as the impulse of shame, into the psyche which would insure that my creator would immediately wish to go back into the creation rather than remain exposed outside it.

"I also placed within its psyche the idea that it could only realize its identity when existing in relation with some manifestations of its own creation. In short, it had no beingness, consciousness, or activity except in connection with objects.

"And since this creator's creations were part of its identity, it could not leave its creation without losing the self, which is the part that strived to escape in the first place, and without which there was no urge to go anywhere or do anything.

"In this way I saved myself the unmentionable and paradoxical problems arising from the efforts of an Absolute Being trying to create subjective and partial objects and creations of limited beings.

"Now I could be sure of a continual stream of creation without having to constantly do everything myself. This system was very economical, because it only required one being. I did not have to populate it ever with one other being, because no other beings needed to be present. Since the entire world picture could be projected around the creator, I could eliminate the need for the creation of a companion. I felt sure that sooner or later the creator would create a little something for himself to keep him company.

"And through careful observation of these creations which were being produced by this perpetual creator of mine I was able to pluck ideas from here and there which had some objective merit, and place them in a new world I am in the process of creating — or more truthfully, assembling out of used parts from the automatically proceeding creation world.

"And to this perpetual creator of mine, the world in which he has been placed appears as a bunch of white clouds unless a reality is proceeding within it.

"When a reality is proceeding, it seems to be a world with

people, and sky, and trees, and sun and mountains and so on. And I called this perpetual creator placed within the creation substance 'man'.

"And the first thing this perpetual creator 'man' did when he was placed in there was to look up at the sky and create a creator. That's right...He created a creator and then invented the idea that that creator was the one who was creating everything around him, and that he was not responsible for any of it — even though the reality was continually adjusting itself to his ideas — and then he simply settled back to watch!

"But it seems now that this creator of mine has somehow managed to overcome the urge to create even automatically, and that he is now becoming able to resist this urge to the point of total stagnation of the world. In short, he has managed to deflect the urge to create by turning it into the urge to rearrange already existing creations. Eventually of course it will all run down into a great amorphous blob.

"So unless we do something about this, my creator will have to be dismantled and I will be forced to find another means for the assemblage of my new world.

"And with that, the Lord sat back and slowly sipped on a mint julep. I could tell what the other angels were thinking. They were thinking it was too bad He was impervious to arsenic.

But be that as it may, we had a real problem. If this creator would not create, how could we get it to create? And if it would not operate unconsciously, what hope was there that it would agree to function consciously? How could we get this creator to agree to assume its cosmic duty? And we did not have a lot of time in which to accomplish this, either...if The Lord was any authority.

The problem as I saw it was not to get the creator willing to perform this obligation, but to get it back to the point at which it was *able* to perform its primary and natural function. It was easy to see that this creator had fallen down in a spiral

from a being that was able to do and to create something out
of nothing, or almost nothing — to a being who was now
not even able to erase the garbage heap of inert mass that
this creation world had become through his inaction and
apathy.

There was something else we all wondered about. Why did
the beings created by this creator — the ones called
'humans' — behave as if they were totally cut off from the
unified consciousness of the creator?

When we discovered that they really were cut off from the
unified consciousness of the creator, we really began to
worry. It turned out that at the first shock generated by the
'Terror of Endlessness' perceived at the first erasure of the
world form, the creator, in order to better hide itself within
the folds of its creations, had shattered itself into many
billions of billions of individual mini-beings, each of which
had established within itself a set of habits forming its
beingness and had gone off on its own for so long now, that
reunification was by this time completely impossible.

As it turned out this was a lucky accident, since this is the
real cause for self-arising of Real Essence Individuals who
have been objective enough to be placed in the new world
being assembled by The Lord.

And so we resolved on a solution which would not require
the reunification of the perpetual creator, but which would
solve once and for all the problem of the apathetic creator
and the vanishing cosmos.

"As I see it," offered Galadriel, "We're working with at
least two problems. The strivings which force the creator to
create, and the over-response in relation to those strivings. I
mean of course the two laws: *Striving To Escape*, and the
Shame Of Nakedness, which are, as we all now know, the
causes of the desire to create and uncreate — to tear down
and break through creation to the zero point, and the desire
to build and enforce in order to hide, respectively."

"Yes," agreed Hadriel. "It's obviously all in this folding

and unfolding process that something has gone wrong.''

''Ah, well, now,'' said The Lord. ''Let's see what this creator of mine is doing right now to avoid the effort of creation...''

We looked inside the creation substance. He was trying to escape by absorbing the white clouds of creation substance.

''He no doubt perceives this process as the reciprocal eating of his own body, and his body being at the same time eaten by the world,'' The Lord commented. ''And he would no doubt feel extreme pain from all this, if not for the deep sleep within which he maintains himself.

''It should produce no pain whatever, as both the body and the surrounding space are made of the same stuff, but in determining the limits of his identity he has decided that his body — which is according to his ideas his 'real self' and the surrounding space — which is according to these same ideas 'not himself' are two separate entities having nothing to do with each other or in common with one another.

''And this eating through the white clouds in order to erase the existing mess brought about by his refusal to consciously create the world around him has become with him only legendary because of the extreme state of sleep in which he exists.

''He now believes that this 'eating of his own body' only occurs philosophically, and refers to it as the 'Holy communion of the Eucharistic Mass', and 'The Seder'.

''That is to say, through his deep hypnosis, he has only a dim perception of the truth of the situation. If he knew the real situation, of course, he would go quite mad. And it was because of this tendency of his to go insane at the perception of his real situation that I created for him the psyche now surrounding his Essence, or Real Self.

''Which all pertains to this perverted and degenerate urge to be continually amused and entertained by the things around him.

''And so, this abnormal but perfectly understandable

response of his toward the reality of the situation has led to
his deterioration as a creator and to his total collapse of all
efforts as a being.

"Which of course eventually means that in the final
absorption of the white clouds he remains alone and
unprotected outside space and time without preparation for
the event.

"And suddenly finding himself alone in the central sky,
surrounded only by the Sun-Absolute and moon, he goes into
a state of shock, since up to then he has been under deep
hypnosis and thus protected from knowledge about all this,
and he responds with the impulse of *Striving To Hide His
Nakedness* by...Ahem...By turning himself inside out.

"And then with a great *Cry of Anguish* he vomits out the
stars and planets, and begins eating his way out of it once
again.

"And so the process of creation has degenerated into a
process of reciprocal feeding, in which no new creation is
possible."

The Lord finished speaking, and a few small thunderhead
clouds formed near Him indicating His unhappiness. A few
tiny crackles of lightning murmured with appropriate
thunder within the depths of the small gray storm.

"But I don't understand, Lord," I said. "Why does this
creator of yours respond so violently in the presence of the
Sun-Absolute?"

"That's the way it was set up. The presence of the Sun-
Absolute was supposed to radiate with love and joy, and
cleanse him of all previous creation, so that an entirely new
creation could be created. But as it turned out, the presence
of the Sun-Absolute was a terrible shock to him, because he
had become attached to the previous creation, and felt
threatened by the Sun-Absolute's radiations which would
erase all traces of the creation he had become so dependent
upon.

"And this is what has caused him to close down and

become dependent upon the substitution of the process of reciprocal feeding instead of his own efforts at the creation of his own world in whatever form suits him at the moment.

"All this indicates to me that his being has become almost completely useless for actual creation. But think what a job it would be to break in a new one. Even then there's no guarantee that something else won't go wrong again. No — we might as well try to salvage this one.

"I guess we could put some buffers up around the Sun-Absolute...But then the striving to reach the Sun-Absolute would not be as strong as it is now...What's the matter? Didn't I mention the striving toward the Sun-Absolute?"

"No, Lord," said Archangel Lefkowitz. "You never said anything about it."

"I suppose I should have told you about it right off," He said, "But it never occurred to me that it might be a problem. But just now it has suddenly been perceived by me that it may very well be the crux, so to say, of the dilemma.

"The striving toward the Sun-Absolute was an idea that I formulated after I noticed that this creator of mine had somehow neglected to respond positively to the impulse of striving to escape.

"And so I thought I would add a more positive and joyous striving to it, to reinforce it and make it more pleasant for this creator of mine to find himself outside his created space.

"But I had not counted on an unforeseen reaction of his, called 'rapture', which is the result of sudden shocking exposure to the presence of the Sun-Absolute, which has been perverted into the experience which the creator now feels instead of the experience of rapture, and which he subjectively senses as 'the result of shame at appearing naked before The Lord'.

"Tell me...How can rapture due to exposure to the vivifying presence of The Lord become transmogrified into the impulse of shame?

"Finally I realized that the impulse of shame was aroused in him as a result of his feeling of remorse stemming from his really quite madcap behavior in substituting the reciprocal process of feeding for conscious creation.

"And he has somehow confused this automatic process of reciprocal feeding with the means of his sexual reproductive process. I have noticed that those thoughts related to sex have been uppermost in his mind when we have occasion to see each other 'face to face' so to speak.

"And during those periods of uncreation just prior to his peculiar action of turning himself inside out those thoughts related to what he calls 'eating' and 'sex' seem to bother him quite a bit.

"He seems to think that they are actions of his which are somehow displeasing to me...And of course they are, but not for the reasons he thinks.

"You can see how upset he is with all this," The Lord continued. "Look there. See how that ball of clouds rolls and folds in on itself? That's how my nickname for his cosmos came about. I call it the 'Samovar' or *self-boiler*."

"But Lord," I interrupted, "All those explanations still have not told us why you decided to create things in the first place."

"Well," said The Lord, looking around at all the Angelic Host and carefully surveying all of the creation as if for the last time, "It seemed like a good way to organize my thoughts...And now, I bid you all...goodnight."